THE DEATH IMPORTER

When a detective is called in to help in a private matter, he does not normally expect to be asked to clear up the mess left by a gory murderer so as to keep the whole thing quiet from the police. In the normal way, Keyes wouldn't have agreed, but just as the beautiful Miss Wiseman had a reason to keep the murder quiet, so the detective had a reason to do as he was asked. But that didn't stop natural inquisitiveness enticing him into further trouble.

JOHN NEWTON CHANCE

THE DEATH IMPORTER

Complete and Unabridged

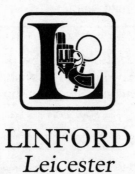

LINFORD
Leicester

First published in Great Britain in 1981 by
Robert Hale Limited
London

First Linford Edition
published 2003
by arrangement with
Robert Hale Limited
London

British Library CIP Data

Chance, John Newton, *1911 – 1983*
    The death importer.—Large print ed.—
Linford mystery library
    1. Detective and mystery stories
    2. Large type books
    I. Title
    823.9'14 [F]

    ISBN 0–7089–9952–2

Published by
F. A. Thorpe (Publishing)
Anstey, Leicestershire

Set by Words & Graphics Ltd.
Anstey, Leicestershire
Printed and bound in Great Britain by
T. J. International Ltd., Padstow, Cornwall

This book is printed on acid-free paper

1

I came to Ravenleigh at around three in the afternoon. The sky was overcast but the air was calm. There was a high red brick wall enclosing the grounds, but the iron gates with rather rusted, fake heraldic signs wrought in in each leaf, were open. The house itself, red brick and stone mullion in mellow Victorian grand style, looked warm and comforting for those inside and a little stern to those outside. There were trees around behind it and to the sides and bordering the expanse of the lawns in front of it. Red and yellow leaves ran uneasily in the small scurries of wind that were beginning to disturb the calm of the scene.

I felt rather sorry that I had not come to this place in response to their call for help some time earlier.

Instead I had been seduced into accepting the van Deken job and landed myself with considerable difficulties.

I had left behind at my flat the beautiful woman, Alexandra van Deken, who insisted on being my wife. I had a fancy that previously she had widowed herself and that was the reason she had gone back to her van Dekenship.

She was very beautiful, some thirty-five years, of outstanding figure and animal grace, and walked about my flat clad in a long, shining black sable coat with nothing on underneath it. That habit caused me restlessness and occasional desperation.

At forty I am in the prime of life, of course, but Alex had the skill of returning me to the prowess of my late teens, which gave me appetites during which I ate like a voracious pig.

Gluttony is a waste of good food, I believe. Alex is a wanton as regards food as well as other matters. Her idea of roast duck sauce is oranges, much brown sugar, lemon, cayenne pepper all boiled in apricot brandy. The result lifts the top off the head, leaving a rosy vacuum. The palate, is of course, numbed for days.

I had chosen the van Deken job

because I had thought it the richer. My first sight of Ravenleigh made me think I could have been wrong.

I leaned back against a tree outside the gates and looked at the house and the grounds for some time, absorbing the atmosphere.

The wind was becoming less pronounced and to the left of the house the sky over the sea was taking on a new colour, purple. As the colour darkened the wind died away and a stillness came.

I walked down to the gates and through on to the drive which led to a terrace up a set of broad stone steps. As I came near, the big main door opened and a woman appeared.

She was big and loose-looking, with a loose gown, and a loose, easy way of standing. She had blonde hair with a bun at the back as I saw when she turned her head to look briefly to one side.

I was not very pleased at the thought of dealing with another woman. I had not shaken off the last commitment and was uneasy at the thought of more involvement.

Perhaps I had been misled by suggestion in the name, 'H. J. Wiseman ', which sounded male. The woman at the door was clearly waiting for me.

'Mr Keyes?' she said, as I approached.

I took off my hat and admitted to the false name. We shook hands.

'I am glad you were able to come at last,' she said. Her mouth, like the rest of her, was big and loose, and there was a half smile when she said the last two words.

I assumed she was around forty in age and bust and not far short of six feet in height. I felt a personal uneasiness for hers was a type by which I am rather easily influenced.

'A short illness intervened,' I said, by way of apology for having done the van Deken case first.

'Do come in,' she said, and smiled again as she turned away; as if hiding something from me, I thought.

It was, as I had sensed, very comfortable inside. I saw nothing of great value in the way of furniture, though all was good.

4

She took me into a room off the hall. It was large, lined with books on three walls, the shelves were broken for a stone fireplace, on the main wall facing the windows. There were leather armchairs with small mahogany tables beside them and a large, matching table with appropriate chairs round it. It was a reader's library, a student's library. Most comforting.

I love to feel surrounded by knowledge which I need not consult.

We sat at the large table, facing each other.

'My father died almost a year ago,' she said.

'Then you are H. J. Wiseman?'

'I'm sorry. I didn't make it clear. Yes. Helen Jane. As I said a moment ago, the matter was not that urgent when I first wrote to you, so that your delay in coming did not matter.'

She paused, as if for me to ask a question.

'It does now?' I said.

'I'm afraid very much so. My problem at first was that my father's will, which he always kept here, was found to be missing.'

'Was there only one copy?' I looked round the room and glanced at the grounds through the window.

'Yes, there was. And yes, it involved a large sum of money together with property.' She smiled almost lazily. 'The answer to the question which you haven't said aloud is that my father did not trust lawyers.

'Every case at law he got drawn into, he defended himself. He had plenty of reference books, as you see.'

She was very charming, very softly pleasant. As my eyes briefly enjoyed the curves of her bosom as she leant against the table, a sable coat seemed to intrude, almost with the gleam of menace as it swept sinuously into my mind.

'My mother died some years ago. I have one brother, and one sister who disappeared in an air crash ten years ago. That was in the Pacific. All seventy passengers and five crew disappeared, though part of the tail of the machine was found a fortnight after.

'So I don't think you need bother with Elizabeth.'

'Ten years is a long time.'

'It is also a long way to swim from the middle of the Pacific to anywhere.'

'And nothing was heard of that flight afterwards?'

'Only the tail of the aircraft.'

'And your brother?'

'My brother is the cause of the sudden urgency,' she said, and sat back and looked at me with clear grey eyes. 'He was murdered about two am this morning.'

'Where?'

'Here.'

I was taken aback. She was watching me and knew what I felt, I was sure of that. She had said it in such quiet tones, no drama, no high feeling, just a quiet soft voice in a tone she might have used for saying the cat was lost.

'I see no signs of police,' I said, and felt a bit edgy.

'I haven't told anyone but you,' she said and leaned back with her arms stretched across the top of the chair.

She looked so serene, so unfettered by

worry that I couldn't believe she was talking about murder.

I did not know what to say. From most other people I would have felt the tension of my leg being stretched, but not from H. J. Wiseman. She was something away from most other people; a long way away.

'The police will have to be told,' I said.

'Oh they will be,' she dismissed them almost with impatience, 'but only when I know exactly what happened. So that it does seem almost heaven sent that you should arrive only a few hours after the discovery.'

I did not know what to do. Not having police to deal with suited me personally, but it also put us into the position of accessories after a murder.

Unless, of course, we found who did it.

Such a discovery might be even more uncomfortable than being an accessory.

'Are you quite sure that this is what you want to do, Miss Wiseman?'

'I'm sure it is the best for me, the family name and my daughter.'

'Your daughter? Oh you are — '

'No, I'm not. I'm one of the Old

School of Thinking for Women. Seek 'em, seduce 'em, sod 'em.'

She smiled again. I was being taken aback with the frequency of a poor boxer.

'My daughter is away at school,' she said. 'I don't want her to walk into an unpleasant mess at half-term next week.'

And what a nasty mess it would be if the child came back to find her mother in jug with her professional detective, held for conspiracy to murder her uncle, aiding concealment, abetting a felony, and/or being accomplices, together with some other charges which came into my mind.

'I didn't mention the fee I propose,' she said. 'You can have anything you like. Money? You say how much. If there is anything about the house of value which you fancy instead, you shall have it. This is not by way of a bribe. When I need help, I pay.'

'Very generous,' I said and sat back to think of the situation from the start. 'I suppose there are servants here?'

'Yes. There is a maid, a cook and a

cook's maid; a chauffeur-handyman-butler sometimes and a gardener.'

'Do they live in?'

'All but the cook. She comes in by car each day. The other four have a wing of the house to themselves. Father's idea.'

I looked at the table top and thought for a while.

'What exactly do you think I can do for you?' I said.

'Just find out who did it. There the matter ends, as far as you're concerned.'

'That must be in theory. In practice it will be impossible.'

I have a disadvantage in that I was once indiscreet and just got away with it, though the Prosecutor's file is still open, one might say, to further suggestion.

I found that the van Dekens had known of this bone in my cupboard, which had proved a great help to them in walking over my conscience and natural thoughts for my safety.

Looking at H. J. Wiseman then I felt she knew about that same bone.

The trouble in such a case is one can

only assume. One cannot ask without giving it away.

'I'll show you what has happened upstairs,' she said, and got up.

★ ★ ★

Following her long, elegant, lazily moving body up the stairs made me wish for quite another reason for going up. In any case, I dislike dead bodies. I get depressed, and that upsets my stomach, which to me means intense mental gloom.

I suppose at that moment I was really hoping that she had made a mistake, and that the brother had been suffering from unconsciousness or a death trance. Both are popular in books.

At the top of the stairs she turned to the right along a passage and opened a door, again on the right, so that the room was in front of the house.

She stood to one side.

'Do go in — carefully,' she said.

I was more than careful; I was slow with distaste. When I got inside the room I stopped and looked around.

11

A horrid taste came into my mouth, probably an uprush of adrenalin common in moments of abject fear.

She came in behind me and closed the door.

'You see ?' she said quietly.

It was impossible not to see. The place was a shambles, a slaughterhouse. There was blood on the tumbled bedclothes, up two walls, on the carpet, and the curtains.

In the midst of this charnel house scene a man lay sprawled in bloody pyjamas on the floor. He seemed to have been hit many times with a sharp, heavy weapon; a chopper or a sword.

The mess was due to the murderer having no idea of how to effect a direct killing, but hitting away until the victim was dead.

The curtains were pulled back. The day outside looked even darker.

'Did you pull the curtains?' I said, trying to swing my attention to anything away from the man on the floor.

'No. He always had the curtains open at night. He said he couldn't breathe otherwise.'

'Where do you sleep?'

'In the other corridor across the landing.'

'There must have been a row going on. Did you hear anything?'

'Yes. It woke me, but I thought it was a noise down in the village. As soon as I was awake it stopped, so I thought no more of it.'

'When did you — er, find — ?'

'About twelve. I came up to tell him he should get up and have his bath. We lunch at one.'

'Did you?'

'I had to pretend. Cook would have wondered.'

'He always got up late?'

'When he was here he did.'

'So nobody came to clean the room as usual?'

'The room got cleaned when the staff knew he was out of it. He used to tell Ann; she usually does our rooms.'

'Who locks the house up at night?'

'Jim, the chauffeur-factotum.'

'Did you ask him if he did last — ? No, I suppose that would have made him wonder if anyone had got in. I see there's a balcony outside each main window up here.'

'They were added in about 1890, I believe.'

'Not difficult to climb up here with a rope and grapple.'

'I'm not a burglar, but I take your word.'

'I can't see any weapon.'

'I couldn't either. You seem rather frightened to move?'

'I am thinking of the police coming in eventually. It's important not to move anything.'

'Then how will you find out who did it?' She smiled in gentle askance.

'I don't propose to do it by leaving my prints over everything.'

'You are quite stern, Mr Keyes.'

'It is a serious matter,' I said earnestly. 'I know you must be upset, but I cannot think what made you decide not to call the police. Really — a thing like this — It needs forensic — pathologists — every modern means of tracking a murderer. I have none of these things.'

'I am very jealous of the family name, Mr Keyes. There are some things I don't want made public.'

'About your brother?'

'Yes. He was an importer.'

'Of what?' I waited and she hesitated quite a few seconds.

'Of drugs. He told me not long ago he was a millionaire already, just from importing.'

'Did he distribute as well?'

'No. It went away to a centre and from there to other centres. A spider's web.'

'This isn't a gang job,' I said. 'This is an amateur bodge-up. A man who started to kill and found it was harder than he thought.'

The words brought such a dreadful picture to my mind I closed my eyes for a moment.

'You mean personal, Mr Keyes?'

'Yes.'

'That's what I thought, and that is why I refrained from calling the police. You see, it could be a friend.'

'A friend? Not his friend!'

'No. He had very few. He was very

self-sufficient, hard. In some ways he was evil. He had no sympathy for human weakness. When he told me what his business really was he did it in place of hitting me physically, which he also sometimes did. That time he wanted to do something that would hurt to last.'

I stared at her in genuine shock.

'I somehow formed the idea that you were fond of him.'

'I was. Yes. As a girl I always admired strength, and he had that. But I believe strength does not last, and that it creates an awful, black loneliness. I believed that one day he would need my sympathy and understanding.

'I let that out, when we were rowing one day. I lost my temper and said so. That's when he retaliated with the truth about his interests.'

'I see. And when was this?'

'A fortnight ago. As the days passed I persuaded myself that he had invented it to shatter me; to keep me at a distance from his affairs. He knew I would never tell anyone.'

'You wouldn't tell if you couldn't

believe it yourself. But if you had believed it you would be too frightened to tell.'

'That's kind of you. But that is the fact.'

'Did he live here most of the time?'

'Yes. It seems the importing was into the coast all round here. Coves, inlets, quiet rivers. That sort of place.'

'So one assumes he kept a lot of money in the house,' I said, with a slight feeling of warmth for the stuff quickening my interest. It directed my mind away from this messy business.

'I suppose he must have done, but I never knew of it.'

'Suppose we leave this for a while and talk about his friends and behaviour lately.'

'If that's best for you,' she said, indicating the door.

She followed me out.

'I have my father's suite,' she said. 'He wished that. We shall talk in there.'

We crossed the landing. She entered the opposite corridor and opened the first door left, again standing back for me to pass her.

17

I went into a large bedroom with a circular carpet and a low, circular silk bed in the middle of that. Hanging on the walls were five Eastern tapestries depicting the most athletic sexual activities in lurid silk colours. They were so beautiful the obscenity of the subjects seemed to be unimportant.

'My father was a merchant, doing large business with the orient,' she said, indicating various statuettes with her hand.

These models, standing around on small tables and columns were even more vigorously active in the pursuit of copulation than the tapestries.

'He had, as you see, a two-track mind,' she said, and led the way through to an adjoining room, furnished as a small drawing room without much erotica, except for some paintings of Western origin.

'Sit down, Mr Keyes. I will get you a drink.'

She went to a cabinet in a corner of the room. I looked out of the window.

For the first time, I think, I had a

feeling of being trapped in this place and the spring of the trap lay in my own precarious legal position.

Acting with her to conceal murder would be the spikes at the bottom of the trap.

She gave me a sherry. I drank it for its wetness rather than its taste. I was surprised to find my throat so dry.

'His friends?' I said.

We sat down. She told me of a few local friends who were clearly her friends or old family friends. She mentioned no close friends of the brother's.

I looked at her very straightly.

'This is an impossible situation,' I said. 'To get anywhere it would be necessary to interview dozens of people, travel around the coast, to the little places, the secret inlets and all the rest of it. And if we can't question the servants for fear of them suspecting — how are we to do anything?'

'Time. There is plenty of time.'

'I don't understand. Don't you intend to call the police at all?'

'No. I have told you already, I am very jealous of the family. I don't want the name plastered all over the plebby blatts, as my daughter calls them.'

'It was fortuitous that I came, you think,' I said, feeling angry and not a little tied up. 'But I wrote to you and said I would be here today. Is it fortuitous that he died last night?'

I thought she would put on the high haughty, the haute affronte; but she began to laugh.

'My dear man! I'm not such a fool as that!'

And looking at her, I found that I began to laugh as well, I suppose as reaction to her charm and a sudden release from my tensions.

The tensions, however, returned when she leant forward, patted my hand and gave that slow half smile right, it seemed, into my eyes.

'You understand what I meant by *time*,' she said, and sat back. 'You see, Mr Keyes — that is rather formal, but leave it for now — whoever did this is, as you say, an amateur and will most probably be quivering with apprehension and waiting to hear.

'What happens, then, if he hears nothing? What will he do, this amateur, if no one seems to take any notice of his work?'

'His uneasiness will increase,' I said, 'but his nightmares won't help us.'

'I think if nothing happens, and everything seems to be normal here, he will come back to see what's gone wrong.'

'A return to the scene is not a certain reaction,' I said. 'Though it is possible. But that room can't be left as it is. Something will have to be done.'

She sipped her sherry and put the glass down.

'Yes. Well, that can be seen to as required. Now I think the best thing to keep things unremarkable, is for you to go to your hotel in the village and think about what I've said tonight.'

'Yes, I do think that's essential,' I said. 'My bags are there. I'll have dinner and think very hard about the whole dreadful thing.'

'Good,' she got up, and the half smile came again as she looked at me. 'And just after midnight, come back here. I will be waiting.'

I thought of the thousand-guinea sable back home cooking sausages and bacon in champagne sauce, and I felt like an amateur stilt walker on a tight rope stretched across the Thames at Westminster.

2

I suppose that for a while I was acutely unhappy at finding myself in a cleft stick through no fault of my own but a dirty past, which was still outstanding.

I sat and looked at Helen Jane Wiseman with a mixture of feelings; a compound of the sexual and the fearful.

'You want me to come back here after midnight — tonight?' I added ' tonight ' in the hope that the excursion might be put off to some other night.

'Yes. Now you have nothing to worry about once you're here,' she said with a quiet assurance which made me uneasier still. 'By a stroke of luck, the cook's maid, little Angela, is getting married tomorrow, and I've given them all the day off for it.'

'Very kind,' I murmured.

'They are driving the seventy miles up tonight, you see.' The slow smile came again. 'As I wanted Jim to enjoy the party properly I said he might spend tomorrow night there and drive back the following morning.

'It will, you see, save the destruction of a car, possibly.'

'The wedding tomorrow seems another fortuitous incident,' I said. 'You knew I would come today and the servants would be at the wedding.'

'Clearing the way for murder of my brother, is a very rude suggestion, Mr Keyes, but naturally you have to consider everything.'

'So they're all going away this evening. What about the cook?'

'She's going with them. I shall be entirely alone when you come.'

Something about the fact that I could not safely refuse made me angry with her assumption of the truth of my position.

'When I come? I'm still considering the matter. I'm not particularly anxious to help you clean up that shambles.'

'But I feel sure you will,' she said and touched my hand again.

'I will do what I can if it helps you. But you do realise that this will aid the murderer? Honour of the family laid aside, I don't see why you should be so keen to save him.'

'His safety is incidental, and, I am determined, will be brief. You will find him, Mr Keyes. It will be difficult but I am quite confident that you will find him.'

Walking away from the house and down the winding path to the harbour, I kept seeing in my mind the bloody scene in that bedroom and wondered why it seemed incongruous as well as horrible.

I think that the reason was that the animal ferocity of the killing did not match the probable stealth and cunning of a person who had got in without anybody having seen him.

The sort of brutal murder which had finished the brother seemed to go with a man who would have smashed the door down first.

But then, drugs change mentalities for brief periods, and the drug link was there in the victim.

I had left my bag and the car at a pub overlooking the harbour. As it was the after-season period the landlord and his wife had gone away for their holidays leaving the place in the hands of a reputedly married couple whose bent was to eat and drink the stock in continuous intake.

The woman, Julie, was plump, peaches and cream and blonde and ate cheese and biscuits and chocolate wafers one after the other, helped only by packets of raisins, nuts and pork crackling strips, out of packets.

The man, George, appeared to be a taster who swallowed the test. He tested every spirit bottle on the shelves at frequent intervals, to make sure they hadn't gone off, I suppose.

He confided to me that he was going to get her on her back by lacing her lemonades with Vodka without her knowing.

When I arrived she was in the bar with five fishermen who were sharing jokes and when she took their drinks to them on a tray, they pinched her bottom and squeezed her breasts and tickled her and made her laugh so that I fancied she'd be on her back without the help of laced-up drinks.

Which suited my purpose, since they would probably be both boozed out of their senses by midnight.

The accommodation was good, simple and made me feel I would miss nothing by creeping out of it.

Dinner was served to me in the private parlour downstairs and was an excellent Irish stew which had clearly been master-minded before George had started his day's lacing.

Julie served it and each time she bent over the table I felt I might be suffocated. Her dress revealed a surfeit of flesh all a-wobble. I would have seen down to her navel but for the great breasts forced together in a bra with the dimensions of a hammock.

This vista was pushed almost into my face frequently when she served something, took it away, or asked something, and she smiled and giggled and winked and presented a danger to my plans.

If she got the idea I fancied her she

could become an obstacle to my intentions.

This fear became more acute when I saw how George was getting on in the bar after I had eaten. He was getting very tight. I feared he was getting so fuddled he was forgetting his intention to lace Julie's drinks.

In the bar she insisted on bringing my drink to me and coming again to wipe my table, and then sat down in the pew beside me and started to talk about the attractions of the season just past. Then she winked and said she could guess what sort of attractions I'd fancy and pinched my knee.

Fortunately, George fell over behind the bar amongst a lot of bottles, by the sound, so she jumped up and ran behind to him.

'Bloody boddle rolled right under me bloody foot!' he shouted from below.

Three customers followed her behind the counter and all but one disappeared from view.

'It's all right, he's not broken anything,' Julie said, and re-appeared, ruffled and red in the cheeks from bending.

They heaved George into view and sat him on the stool from which he had fallen. While this activity went on I noticed a young man watching me.

He was standing against the wall by a window looking out on to the harbour lights. He was thin, shock-tow-headed, wore gold rimmed spectacles and stared morosely at me. He wore a denim jacket, old jeans and gumboots. There was an old army gas mask satchel slung from his shoulder. He had a tankard in his right hand.

While the rescuers were patting George and stopping him from coughing by slapping his back and almost knocking him off the stool again, the young man came across to me.

He sat on a bench on the other side of my table, put down his beer and nodded to me as he reached into his breast pocket.

'Not a bad night,' he said, and brought tobacco and cigarette papers from the pocket. 'Know this place?'

I said, 'No. Taking a few days' rest.'

'I thought I might get work here,' he said, rolling without looking up. 'You wouldn't know, then?'

'I'm afraid not. What do you do?'

'Repair boats. Chippie. Do engines as well. I heard there was a man wanted so I came. Bloody place is shut up. The feller owns it's gone away.'

He shrugged and licked the cigarette paper along, watching me through the glinting gold frames.

'Bad luck,' I said.

He shrugged again.

'Would have been an easy number, I reckon. Nice quiet shop, up the creek over the head.' He jerked his head backwards to indicate the headland.

'You mean a boathouse — a yard?' I said.

'Private. You know,' he said. 'Shouldn't think there's many customers. Does it all for himself. Wiseman, the name. Know him? Big house way up on top. Went up there to ask. Saw a woman. His sister, it was. Fine woman.' He shook his head in sad appreciation of the fineness. 'Reckon she could do you a power of good on a stormy night.'

He didn't smile. Just looked wistful.

'You putten up here?' he said, lighting the cigarette at almost the same time, like a ventriloquist.

'Just for tonight.'

I was wondering why he had picked on me to talk to. He seemed to be after something and that, for many reasons, made me uneasy.

He had also met Helen and heard that Wiseman had gone away, and there was the boathouse and its need for a boat repairer, which sounded pointed, somehow, as if he were prodding me to say I knew something about it.

I knew nothing about a boathouse until he had mentioned it. The existence of such a building made it seem that Wiseman might have been running the smuggling boats himself.

If that was the case, then the crewmen would be somewhere around, waiting for orders from him.

His talk made unhappy listening to me. Helen J. had made no mention of a boathouse, nor of any crews. If the dead brother had had men about who were waiting for messages from him, then the whole Wiseman situation began to appear to be one to get right away from.

He kept watching me as if expecting me to say something about his work, the boathouse or the woman at the big house.

Perhaps I looked a bit sharp, for he shrugged and sat up straight.

'Sorry to stare,' he said. 'But I feel I've seen you before somewhere.'

'It's always possible,' I said. 'You travel a bit, do you?'

'I follow the work,' he said. 'Get a job, stay at it till I get a bit sick of the surround, then move on.' He looked round. 'Time I got a bed fixed. Bit late now to look round the town. Better ask her.'

He got up.

My unease grew. I had the feeling that he had decided to stay near me.

★   ★   ★

I went out and walked round the harbour. It was very still, the sea like satin under the quay lights. If a storm was coming, it was hanging back a long time. The air was warm but there was that slight touch of cold on the nostrils that smelt like rain.

At that time I was thinking in terms of drama. I had been snared at the big house. I had come to a pub with an atmosphere which was taut with the signs of impending disaster. I had been sought out by someone who seemed to sense what I knew.

Could he be a plain-clothes man? An agent? A customs detective?

Did someone know what had happened at the house last night? That was possible.

Despite their usual custom, one of the servants might have looked into that room and seen the mess. But if they had, why had there been no commotion at the time? Were they all crooks, each concerned in his own crime so that he wouldn't have made the murder known for personal business reasons?

But it would be impossible, surely, that a person could suddenly have come upon such a scene and not been knocked backwards?

Yet Helen Jane Wiseman had done just that. Calmly, unconcernedly, she had closed the door and gone down to lunch.

She had been without any sign of worry or anxiety when I had called at that place, yet in her mind must have been the lurid picture of that room upstairs, just as it had stayed in mine since it had hit my eyes.

I came to the end of the harbour wall and sat on an iron bollard to sort my head out, and think of the immediate need for planning.

My way out of the pub later had already been decided. I had a side window to my bedroom and below there was the roof of a long shed which backed on to an alley. I could see no difficulties in using that way out, and back.

But there were two possibilities which led to fearful thoughts.

The first, that the boat mender might be parking himself in the pub specifically to watch me.

Second, and less easily dodged, was the

amorous Julie, and I was sure I knew what she had made up her mind would happen. Her husband was already drunk; she could attack free of his interference.

If she decided to come to my room after midnight, then I was as good as shopped, because I wouldn't be there.

A humorous thought passed in my mind lightening my gloom momentarily. It was just that Julie had been lacing George's drink so he had forgotten to lace hers.

That brief light was extinguished by the thought that, even if I got out and up to the house without trouble, our job was to clean up that terrible room.

There was one point I had to make when I got there, and that was when washing blood from the walls and floor, furniture and anything else, the bloody water can splash on to one's clothes and leave enough of the stuff to be detected later.

There are far too many clever little dodges in the forensic laboratories these days. Not that their conclusions are always right, but if they lead to a hand on the shoulder, right or wrong doesn't matter.

Watching the lights moving lazily on the water below me and hearing the soft lap of sea against the wooden sides of the moored boats, soothed my mind.

My thoughts drifted away to worlds where there was less immediate pressure, more time for pleasure.

Then suddenly that black sable coat swirled angrily, like a ghost dancing up and down over the water, arms waving in reproof and warning, dancing 'The Indignant, the Possessive, The Demanding.'

I sighed. Were things ever slow and easy and free of pressure? What had I done to deserve this torment?

Everything.

I went slowly back to the pub.

George was leaning heavily on the bar telling stories to a group of free drinkers gathered round him. They were laughing at him and nudging each other where he couldn't see.

The boat builder came up to me, a tankard still in his hand.

'Have a drink?' he said, glumly.

I accepted and caught Julie's eye. She was staring merrily at me and winked when I looked. She broke off to serve the boatman.

I sat down. He came back with the drinks.

'I fixed a bed,' he said. 'For myself, I hope.' He indicated Julie with his eyes. 'A nympho.'

'A hipponymph,' I said. 'I dare say she would be suitably enthusiastic.'

'Oh, it's quite a proposition,' he said, watching her serve. 'The only thing is that dopy bugger's going to come to, sometime in the night. I don't like scenes. I like a good sleep afterwards.'

'Will you move on tomorrow?'

'I don't know. That boathouse is still a proposition. I might hang around. I mean, boat business doesn't disappear overnight. You see what I mean, Mr — ?'

I hesitated but there was no point.

'Keyes.'

'Mine's McGuffy.'

'I thought that was a name for a mislead.'

'Pardon?'

He watched me curiously. Again I wondered if he was a plant, sent to the place by somebody who knew me, or knew the Wiseman Group and wanted all the connections.

I was very uneasy in my mind. Over-suspicious.

Over the bar a brass ship's bell was suspended. Suddenly George reached up, grabbed the rope hanging from the clapper and began to ring the bell with such fury it sounded like an ancient fire engine running loose.

'Get out! Go home!' he shouted and added other variations of a less polite kind.

The bell hangings, unable to stand a man swinging on the end, gave way and some of the ceiling and the bell descended on George, who once more disappeared behind the counter wearing the bell as a small hat.

Julie reprimanded him in fish porter's language, but then cleared out the customers efficiently with cheerful smiles, jocular remarks, pushes, pinches and slaps.

She slammed the door after the last one, leaned against it for a moment and went 'Phew!'

George appeared behind the counter covered in plaster and bits.

'That bloody bell fell on me! I'll sue 'em. That's what! I'll have 'em for ten thousand! I'll — '

'You'd best get to bed,' she said very firmly. 'Leave the clearing-up.'

He sort of pushed the top of his head at her as if about to butt her in the midriff.

'Is there blood?' he said urgently.

'You can't get blood out of a block of wood!' she said. 'Now go and wash and go to bed. I'll clear up.'

He staggered off, clutching the door-post for support as he went into the back of the house.

She began to gather up glasses and carry them to the bar.

'He gets so bloody drunk. It's only because they're away. He works proper enough but he can't be trusted on his own.'

'Let me give a hand,' I said, getting up.

'That's very kind,' she said and the light of anger in her china blue eyes changed to a glint I could not mistake.

But what else could I do? Sit there and watch her doing manual labour right under my nose? I don't come from that kind of family.

But she mistook the act, of course. I could see the sable coat right behind me waving its arms like a bat in eager misunderstanding, and then suddenly I could feel the touch on the back of my hand and see the slow, loose-lipped smile of Helen Jane Wiseman.

I was surprised, because such had been the confusion of my shocked emotions at the house, I hadn't really thought she might have the same lecherous thoughts about me as I had had at our first meeting, about her.

I am not usually so surprised, but I am not usually asked, in such a charming and casual manner, to help, illegally, clear up a bloody murder.

I do hate splitting infinitives, but I think that one is arguable, though I have long forgotten all the rules about things like that.

As I carried glasses for her and mopped the tables and generally acted potman and cleaner, McGuffy sat there smoking one of his rolled cigarettes and looking disinterested.

Very soon it was all straight. Julie got my wrist and squeezed it.

'You are kind,' she said, smiling promisingly into my eyes. 'You must have a little drink with me.'

To my relief, McGuffy, who hadn't done anything, got a little drink as well. We sat round for a while talking while the thuds, crashes and bangs of George trying to get into bed, made the lamps shiver on the ceiling beams.

As we chatted, the time rolled on till well after eleven and I began to feel strung up.

If I said I would go to bed, I feared she would close down and come up as well and any chance of making my exit that night would be gone.

Her talk was animated, but McGuffy remained obstinately dull. My hopes for him taking on the responsibility of Julie faded when I thought of his concern for George.

I sat on for a while talking and wishing she would get a headache.

At eleven twenty-seven there was a knocking at the door. Julie made some remark, then got up and slightly opened a window next to the door.

'Oh it's you, Trevor,' she said, quietly welcoming.

My heart rose at the thought that an outside cavalry had arrived for my rescue, then sank again.

'It's all right. They're staying. Been giving me a hand, that's all. George isn't well. Want one yourself? No? Well, okay then, dear. Bysey bye.'

She closed the window and turned back to us.

'The fuzz,' she said. 'Nice boy, though. Throws a good dart. Now then — another for beddy-byes?'

McGuffy, rolling another cigarette, looked up at her as he licked it along. He nodded without stopping the lick.

When she came back with more drinks it was twenty to twelve. Things were getting so sticky that one brief hope lingered in the fact that he had looked at her, although without interrupting his work of rolling.

There had been a silence above for some few minutes.

'Your husband has got to bed, judging by the peace overhead,' I said.

'He'll sleep till morning,' she said, cosily. 'Never fails.'

She smiled down at her drink, hoping to look shy, I thought, cruelly. I touched McGuffy's ankle with my shoe. He looked up at me slowly, eyebrows raised, then at her.

I had both wrists on the table, fingers holding my glass. I looked into my glass hoping McGuffy would make the action. Instead her fingers touched my wrist, then gripped it in a soft grasp.

In my drink I saw the sable coat swirling round like a drowning person spinning slowly in a whirlpool, and the slow smile going down into the glassy funnel with it.

But suddenly the slow, loose, soft-lipped smile stopped going down and rose up and the touch on my wrist was the hand of Helen Jane Wiseman.

I looked up into Julie's laughing, eager eyes.

'I can't sleep with him when he's in that state,' she said.

3

I felt Julie's fingers on my wrist and listened to her softly explaining why she couldn't sleep with her husband that night. In my tortured mind I imagined myself suffocating in the pleasures of her vast bosom while behind her I could see the slow smile from the big house up on the hill, growing wider and showing teeth, and not with pleasure. Behind that still stood the sable coat, handless arms on hips in anger, and I thought of rolling pins and through them to kitchen knives.

I felt myself being misunderstood by Fate. I was being dealt bad hands for weeks on end and trying to stack cards against Fate in person is a waste of cerebral time.

I glanced at McGuffy, sitting thoughtfully beside me, and wondered how I could shift my immediate load of womanhood on to him. Yet he sat there as if the matter was of no interest to him.

The time was passing. I had intended to get out of the pub just after twelve, but as we sat there it was twenty to twelve and moving fast.

Sometimes I wish I was a woman, and I did then, just for the excuses available, like a headache, sleepiness, backache, or the wrong time. For a man to make excuses is not on. In fact history shows it can be dangerous and sometimes lethal. A woman, it seems to me, does not cheapen herself by pushing, only by being turned down.

I suspected that turning down Julie would be, at the least, noisy, and at the most, painful.

McGuffy took no notice when I gave him a light kick on the ankle, it was as if he had a wooden leg.

I sank lower into despair until it seemed that the only way for me was to concede defeat, accede to her demands and steal away once she was asleep.

Helen Jane Wiseman was going to be very cold about that.

Despair gave way to anger at being shoved into such a position, and I blamed

McGuffy. Any man with spirit would have kept to his word and leapt into bed with Julie without hanging about staring at the wall.

Unless he was waiting to see what I would do.

Unless he was watching me and that was what he was here for.

If I once got shut in a room with the Amorous Bulge, I thought he reckoned he could relax his watchfulness and go to sleep.

Then like the trumpeting of The Cavalry beyond the Western hills, a series of thumps and bumps sounded from upstairs.

George was awake. Rescue was at hand.

Julie sat up straight.

'He's fallen out of bed,' she said, then relaxed again. 'He'll sleep where he lands.'

'On the floor?' McGuffy said, stamping out his soggy cigarette end in an ashtray.

'Well, he hasn't come through the ceiling, dear, has he?' she said and shook with laughter. 'Well, I suppose it's time we were off to bed — ' She looked at me.

'Jule! Jule!'

The plaintive shouts from above were accompanied by a thumping on the ceiling which made the lamps being to swing again.

The suspense was unbearable.

She got up and went to the door behind the bar counter. She shouted up the stairs.

'What's the matter?'

'Me edd!' came the desperate cry. 'It's ringing! Ringing! I can't hear anything but ring — ring — ring — Come up, Jule! I think I cracked it! Me *edd*!'

She looked back at us and sighed.

'I'd better say goodnight, by the feel of it,' she said.

We heard her go upstairs. I got up.

'I'll be glad to get some sleep,' I said. 'I just hope he doesn't go off again.'

'He'll keep waking up,' McGuffy said and got up. He stretched his arms to the ceiling beams.

'How do you know?' I said, struck by the oddness of the remark.

'I stuck a bug behind his ear,' he said calmly, and brought a small radio from his pocket. 'I flick this switch. It screams behind the ear. So he keeps awake while I want.'

I stopped by the door and stared at him.

'But why, exactly?' I asked.

'Like I said, I'm a bit wary of that pound of flesh just gone upstairs. I think she needs keeping out of trouble.'

'But what is that contraption?'

'It's an intercom I've been trying to sell. Handy. Even the deaf can hear it — ' he shrugged, ' — but nobody wants it. I just make it oscillate and he gets the scream.'

'I see. Party tricks.'

'If you like.'

'Goodnight.' I went upstairs to my room. Before I went inside I listened and could hear George and Julie talking, or arguing. I thought she sounded angry.

Once in I went to lock the door, but there was no key inside or out. There was a small bolt at chest level. I shot it then went and sat on the bed.

A clock in the town started to chime midnight.

McGuffy was no plain boat mender. The radio gadget had convinced me that my earlier suspicion of him had been well sited.

The trick of sticking a small bug behind a drunken man's ear was not that difficult, perhaps, but, however numbed with drink the victim, such an act would still need speed and skill.

It was possible, I thought momentarily, that he was a small-time inventor and practical jokes man, but the way he had picked on me to talk to, instead of a dozen others in the bar made me sure he was after knowing what my business was.

Again, when he had started talking he had led directly with the boathouse and Wiseman and the big house. That could have been coincidence, but taken in conjunction with the other two points, I couldn't see it like that.

I crossed the room and opened the side window which looked down on to the shed roof. Leaning out, it was possible to see to the left and the harbour, and it was clear that if anybody happened to be out there he would have a clear view of me getting down on to the roof.

Crossing to the windows looking out to the front I could see the whole sweep of the little harbour, and make sure no one was about out there.

I waited until nearly twelve-thirty when all was quiet in the house, then went and looked out through the front windows. There was no one in sight.

The night was still and heavy, an atmosphere that made any sound outstanding. I went to the side window and looked out briefly to make sure no one was in the alley beyond the shed, then climbed out and dropped on to the shed roof.

There was an uneasy silence everywhere. I crossed the roof to the alley and looked one way, then the other before I dropped down into it.

A brief look back at the pub showed no light in any window.

Well, if she came tapping on my door, there was the bolt, and of course, I am a very heavy sleeper. The thoughts came easily as I went away from the place.

★ ★ ★

On my way up the hill and into the grounds of the big house I saw nobody, which was a relief. If I had spotted anyone, I would have dived behind a tree or a bush until they'd gone.

When she opened the door to me I thought for a moment she had changed her mind about our work that night. She wore a dressing gown.

'Did you see anybody?' she said.

'No.'

'Good.' She turned to the stairs. 'I've got things ready upstairs.'

'Before we go — ' I said.

She turned back in enquiry.

'What are we to do with *him*?'

She smiled in apparent relief.

'We have a family tomb down in the wood. One of my grandfather's quirks. We also have a coffin carrier which was supposed to be wheeled along solemnly by the servants and staff in feudal fashion.'

'I see.'

My inside was beginning to move uneasily, as if about to turn over.

We went up the stairs and turned along the corridor to the death room. Outside it there was a chair, buckets, mops, cloths, brooms and other appliances. There were also two pairs of gumboots standing side by side.

She stopped by the chair and put her hand on the handle of the bedroom door.

'Get your clothes off,' she said. 'We want no stains or marks we can't wash off. Take them all off. Cleaners, scourers, dried blood, they could all leave marks on clothes so don't wear any.'

It was very sensible, but cleaning up after a murder, in the nude with a woman, seemed to have some sort of psychological twist about it.

However, I ruminated on the promise of the pay or choice in lieu as I stripped, and it took my mind off immediate problems for a few seconds.

I put on the gumboots. She slipped off the gown and put on the gumboots. I looked the other way to save embarrassment for myself.

She opened the door and we took in the buckets and tools and set them down.

'The curtains are drawn tight,' she said. 'No light will show outside.' She looked at the man messed up in the bedclothes on the floor. 'First, get him into the box.'

I then saw a long wooden box standing alongside the bed. It wasn't six feet long, but wider than a normal coffin, and with straight sides had stencilled on it, 'Parmenter USA'.

'Arms manufacturers,' I said.

'Yes, it held guns, so it's strong.' She took the lid off and laid it across the bed. 'We'll have to bend him a bit. He's flaccid now. I suppose it goes off after a few hours.'

'Yes,' I said, and wondered how many hours it took before *rigor* set in, and how long it lasted.

We unsorted the bedclothes and lifted him into the box.

'Take him outside,' she said, when the lid was on.

We carried out the makeshift coffin and laid it across a table against the wall, which had been cleared for the purpose of serving as a bier stand.

My tensions were slightly relieved. It had not been so dreadful as I had feared. Rather like carrying a wax-work figure about.

We went back into the room, and this time I decided to move things about and have a look here and there for any sign of who might have done it.

My confidence in her belief that the murderer would turn up to see what had gone wrong was not marked, though the possibility did exist — if the murder had been a spur of the moment business.

And the killer had not been a habitual crook.

She pulled off the remaining bed-clothes, bundled them all together and carried them out of the room. Nothing fell out of them.

With those gone, the floor was clear and it was even clearer that there was no axe lying about and no other sort of instrument either.

Apart from the bloodstains on the carpet and walls, there wasn't much damage that I could see.

When she came back I said, 'You know we can't clean the carpets.'

'There's blood on the foot of the bed carpet only,' she said. 'That can be got rid of. Do you see any other stains on the rugs? I can't.'

I could not, though I looked carefully, walking round the bed to make sure.

It seemed that the murderer had appeared at the foot of the bed, and Wiseman had jumped up to get at him and had been pulled over the footboard on to the carpet.

'Better start washing,' she said. 'I hope it won't take long.'

We began washing the walls.

'From all appearances,' I said, rubbing a difficult stain on the plaster, 'your brother saw the man when he was at the foot of the bed. As the windows were all open — or at least one was, it's almost certain the man came up over the balcony. He probably went the same way.'

'Well?'

'This chap knew his way about, and he must have known your brother was in bed, so I think he waited out on the balcony until he was sure of that.'

'It looks that way.'

'Then it doesn't look as if he came to kill him, but just to talk, with the victim at a disadvantage in bed.'

'Possibly.'

'If that was the case, your brother tried to leap forward in the bed, dragging the clothes with him and the killer struck at once.'

'It looked like that.'

'But surely he didn't come with an axe?' I said. 'An unwieldy weapon to carry when rope climbing, unless you were a fireman with a belt sling.'

'It may not have been an axe. A sword, perhaps, or something — ' She stopped then and went on washing.

'Why did you stop? Have you got any swords here?'

'Yes, three or four. Along in the junk room now. Father brought them back from his travels at various times.'

She didn't seem greatly interested.

'Would you know if one was missing?'

'Not really.'

She was hedging the subject, I felt. She had said 'sword' without realising it and afterwards didn't like it.

The swords could be seen after we had finished. We went on rubbing and scrubbing.

It came into my mind that now the cleaning-up was going along fast, she would willingly forget the whole thing once it was done and the box put in the tomb.

The latter job reminded me that there was a lot to do yet, and I felt flattened.

The tension of hiding murder and all that it might mean afterwards had given way to a sort of dull depression.

We had nearly done our job when the quiet of the night was broken by a terrifying sound.

For a moment I could not believe I was actually hearing it; the distant noise must be a figment of my imagination, a ghost of fear.

She became still and looked at me.

'It's the main doorbell,' she said.

She was standing near the wall switches, and turned off the lights.

'You can see down from the balcony. Take a look. Be careful.'

As I turned in the darkness to where I knew the nearest window was, I began to realise that being made an accomplice to a murder, as I had been, was on the way to destroying my independence.

She had ordered me to go and look. Ordered. Had not the situation been as taut as it was I would have resisted her.

In the circumstances I had to do as she ordered, because I needed to look down at the caller.

The edge of the curtains was difficult to find and before I found the opening and went through, the bell downstairs rang again.

That second time of hearing it made me wonder how the first had seemed so terrifyingly loud, for the noise was far away in the bowels of the house.

The night was still outside and there was no light except for that which filtered through the fanlight above the main door from the faint night light in the hall.

Taking care not to show myself I peered down between the stone balusters of the balcony and got an angled view of the terrace before the front of the house.

In the heavy darkness all round the bluish light from the fan seemed quite bright. By it I could see a figure below.

It was a man, standing with his back to the door. At first I thought he was holding his belly with his hands, but then I realised he had got them in the front pockets of jeans.

A slow, creeping fear began to move in me as the man turned and looked at the door, then raised his face and looked along the front of the house, one way and then the other.

The light was too dim for me to be sure, but the shape and posture of the man made me feel that it was McGuffy.

He turned away from the door and I felt a great surge of relief as I saw him walk away from it to the steps down to the drive.

But he stopped, and so did my nervous system. He looked round at the house once more, then it looked as if he shrugged and began to do something with his hands.

I knew what he was doing. He was rolling a cigarette.

His match flared brightly in the heavy night, and the blue smoke wafted up suddenly visible as it came into the soft glow from the fanlight.

He spun the match away across the grass and then got down and sat on the step, his chin almost resting on his knees. He sat there smoking.

I felt my way between the curtains and went back into the room.

'Who was it?' she whispered.

'A man. He was staying at the pub.' I described McGuffy. 'He said he called here today — or yesterday, rather.'

'He did.' Her voice was soft and slow. 'He said he was after a job at the boathouse. Wanted my brother. I said we employed no one down there any more. I wondered how he knew about the boats.'

'Well, he isn't after a job at the boathouse now,' I said. 'He's sitting out there on the steps, smoking.'

She just said, 'Hell!' in an unpleasant little whisper.

'I had an idea he was after something, and not a job at a boathouse,' I said. 'I thought he was after me.'

'Perhaps he knew you came up here just now.'

'He might have guessed. But why follow me up here?'

And then a queer, cold idea came to me. It seemed to come slowly, as if someone had left a door open in my head and chill air had begun to creep in.

Perhaps her intuition was right.

Perhaps McGuffy was the axeman.

But reason pushed the chill a bit offside. If he was morbidly drawn to the scene of the crime, or just curious to know why nothing had happened, he would hardly ring the doorbell at two a.m., and receiving no answer, sit on the step out there to wait.

To wait for what?

For daylight?

Or for me to go out to get back to the pub?

His actions out there seemed to fit in with his desire to talk to me at the pub. They began to paint a picture of a man obsessed with finding out about me and what I was doing in that place.

He waited patiently out there, knowing I would have to get back to the pub before daylight or else raise a lot more questions about my behaviour down there.

Once Julie and George had something peculiar to talk about, I could be sure every customer in the bar next day, and then everybody in the village, would know I was a mystery man, probably a burglar who crept out at night to rob big houses.

To say my business at Ravenleigh would be bust wide open would be understatement; it would be blown apart.

Of course, there was the simpler gossip motive of stealing out at night to seduce the lady of the manor, but everybody round must know that the lady of the manor, if in need of copulation, would have ordered somebody to come for the night, or week.

The idea of creeping out of the pub at midnight could only be put down as an alibi, which was what was intended.

'The room's nearly done,' she whispered. 'It doesn't matter till tomorrow. All the stained stuff is out and we'll deal with it then.'

'Where is it?'

'In a dirty linen basket in the laundry room. Out of sight.'

'What the hell has he come for?' I said. 'Why is he waiting?'

'Take another look. He might have gone.'

Once again I went out on to the balcony, taking good care to make no sound at all. When I peered down through the balusters I saw his back as he squatted on the steps, quite motionless; a statue of patience.

Back in the room, she opened the door and the soft night light of the corridor seemed bright after the dark.

She had cleared up efficiently and all that remained of our activity were our clothes on the chair.

And — regrettably — the armament box.

'Bath,' she said. 'Don't touch anything as we go and follow me.'

'You don't propose to go out after him?' I said.

'No. When we're dressed we've got to get that box down to the tomb.'

I felt myself go cold all through.

4

'Do you mean we should try to take that coffin down to the tomb with that man sitting outside the front door?' I said, following her up the corridor.

'He is sitting on the front steps,' she said, over her shoulder. 'The hand hearse is at the back.'

'It's a quiet night,' I said, in a quiet, strained voice — or so it felt when I spoke. 'Sound carries.'

'It's a long way from the front to the back of this house,' she said, going into her room where a soft light was on and the heavy curtains drawn tight shut. 'Get in the shower.'

She pointed to a door in the wall almost behind me. I went to the door and looked back to ask a question, which I now forget.

With the tensions and uneasiness of the whole affair in the bloody room I had not realised emotionally that we had worn nothing but gumboots. Whether it was the erotic scene of the room behind her or what, I don't know, but the forced remissness of that stretched-out time was suddenly cured.

I went into the bathroom instead of asking the question. She had put everything ready. I went into the glass and tile cubicle and washed off thoroughly, dried and went out again.

She stood in the same position, obviously so as not to touch anything.

'Okay,' she said. 'Get your clothes and take another look down. He might have gone.'

I went into the corridor, along to the chair and dressed quickly, taking care not to look in the direction of the arms box. That done I went back into the room, which caused me no dread now that the corpse had gone.

When I first peered down through the balcony balustrade my heart surged, for he was not sitting on the step. Just to make sure I straightened and looked over the top. It was not quite so dark as it had been, and I thought there might be a glow of the moon somewhere behind the cloud banks.

Despite my sudden rise in spirits, I did not feel quite sure, and looked down by the front door again. He was not there, either.

I turned to go back in but then a shadow caught the corner of my eye and I looked back across the top of the door below me.

There was a moving shadow down there beyond the glow from the fanlight. Someone was walking along the terrace coming away from the end of the house towards the door.

There was little doubt in my mind that McGuffy, tired of sitting doing nothing, had gone to have a look round the side of the house, possibly searching for signs of a lighted window.

He came back to the front door, and then I thought he might have seen such a sign of life.

He rang the bell again and waited, as before, with his hands stuffed down the front pockets of his jeans.

Clearly he knew someone was in the

house and he didn't mind waking them up. That sounded like urgent business, but he had wasted time sitting around smoking cigarettes on the steps out there.

That bellringing looked more like intimidation than any other business. He had come to frighten Miss Wiseman, because he knew what she was up to.

And if he knew that, I felt sure he knew I had got involved in it as well.

Feeling so sure that must be the truth — as I had suspected from the time he first chose to talk to me — I more or less accepted it in my mind.

The question that followed then was: whose side was he on?

If on the side of the law, he would have told his suspicions to the police and left them to get on with it — if, indeed he had enough to convince them.

But if he was on the crook side, such as on the blackmail beat, then we would have to deal with him ourselves.

I did not like that idea at all.

He backed a few paces to get a wider view of the door, as if that might help him see through it to someone hiding on the other side.

He turned his head from side to side after a half minute, looking either way along the front of the house as if wondering which was the best way to go to reach the back of it.

He started to walk off right under the balcony I was on, making slowly for the other corner of the house. I backed through the curtains and went out into the corridor.

She was coming along from her room, buttoning a raincoat. I told her what I had seen. She frowned in an irritated sort of way, but certainly not a frightened one.

'Bloody nuisance,' she said. 'He probably thinks my brother is still here.'

I hadn't thought of that possibility, only that he knew the *dead* brother was here.

'I'll look,' she said, and went into the brother's room.

I waited, and thought I could hear the very faint sound of his whistling out on the terrace.

He was much too cool a customer for my liking. Either that or he didn't realise what he was doing.

As I stood there the bell rang again. He had come back to the door. It was like a persecution.

She came into the corridor about a minute later.

'He's gone and sat on the steps again. Let's get this box downstairs. We've got to get it safely in the tomb before light. There's a road past the wall down there, a wall with railings you can see through.'

'How do we get it down? Not the main stairs?' I said.

I tried to think of my lush reward when this was over, and the gross injustice of the punishment I should get if I didn't go on. These fortified me.

'There is a lift opposite father's room. He was once told he would lose the use of his legs. He didn't, he reckoned, because he had the lift put in first. Cheated fate, he said.' She smiled then. 'He liked cheating Fate. Don't you?'

'If paid,' I said, I think, coldly.

The top of the box was fixed with hasps and hooks. She took four small padlocks out of the table drawer and locked it all securely before throwing the keys back in the drawer.

'They'll be lost later,' she said.

We carried the box to the door opposite the erotic room and lowered it on to a table there. She seemed to have placed everything beforehand. It was all so cool, so practical, so unfeeling.

The door opened outwards.

'We never use it,' she said, conversationally. 'It isn't worth the trouble, except for heavy stuff.'

The inside of the lift was big enough to take a wheelchair and an attendant, but not big enough to take the coffin.

'Stand him up,' she said.

Putting it that way turned my stomach over. I had been trying to think of our burden as a heavy box. She made it sound like the dead male it really was.

We got the box and put it upright. The load shifted inside it, so for a moment I thought I would be sick. I saw her face, and in the moment realised she was almost on the point of laughing at me.

At the bottom we lifted it out into the hall, right behind the door where McGuffy was sitting. I wondered if he would take it into his head to climb up the door and look through the fanlight to see if anyone was about.

She did not speak but indicated which way to go with her head. The door to the back stood open for us. Everything seemed to be arranged for us like that; even a cell door at the end, I thought, as we went through.

We laid the box on another table arranged in the passage. She went back and closed the door into the hall.

The soft night lights were on in this part of the house as well. When we took up the box again I felt it was heavier than when we had put it down.

In my head I reckoned it that the corpse and the box weighed two hundred-weight, and that increased the weight of the load at once.

By tilting the box to my end, I had the major part of the load and began to feel my arms lengthening and my legs being compressed like concertinas.

But for the pain, the whole thing could have been a frightful nightmare as we trudged along a corridor that began to stretch for miles, until it seemed practically endless.

When I was about to plead for a rest, a terrifying sound ripped through my nerves like a laser. The doorbell rang again, right into my ear, it seemed, a thunderous clangour like the beating of a gong pressed against my head.

I almost dropped my end of the box.

'Put it on there,' she said, breathlessly. 'We must rest.'

We lifted the box down onto an old kitchen table placed by the wall. I could hardly see it for sweat in my eyes.

I leant against the table and mopped my face.

'How much does he weigh, for heaven's sake?' I said.

'It's the weight of the box as well,' she said, breathing slow and deep. 'It's not far now.'

'What is the matter with that idiot?' I said.

'Don't let him rattle you,' she said, shortly. 'That's his game. My brother sometimes got funny-head visitors in the middle of the night.'

'Junkies?'

'Probably. Anyhow, he's staying by the front door. Once we have this on the handcart it'll be easy.'

'It's quiet?' I said anxiously.

'Hearses have to be. Otherwise it upsets the sobbing will-chasers. I wonder who that fellow is? He had an odd manner when he called. As if nothing really mattered.'

'That is it. But he bugged the landlord. That takes skill.'

I wiped my face again and looked along the passage. It was not far to go. On the wall, a little way off towards the back, was an old fashioned electric bell indicator, and because of the recent ringing, the disc was still wobbling in its marked hole.

My sight is good. My heart responds very quickly by stopping a moment, then skipping on at pace when shocked. I leaned off the table and went to look closer. The hole in which the disc wobbled was labelled, BACK DR.

★ ★ ★

When I went back and told her she clicked her tongue as if slightly annoyed. Her eyes narrowed as she looked towards the back door and I would not have noticed any special emotion but for the remark she made in a quiet voice.

'I'll screw that bugger's head off!'

It made me glad she was, after all, human. It heartened me so that I did not feel quite so much the lackey as I had done up till then. I had been overborne by her mastery and the involvement in the unpleasantness which she had caused.

'What now?' I said. 'You know the geography. Is the handcart at the back door — close to it?'

'No. It's in a small loading bay the coal truck backs into. But the opening's in full view of the back door.'

'Any lights there?'

'No.'

'Show me. We can see what he's doing, then see what's the best course for us.'

Leaving the box, we started, and as we went, the bell rang again. It was very loud in that passage. Automatically I looked back at the indicator, then stopped in my tracks.

The disc shook in the hole marked FRONT DR.

I put my hand on her arm and pointed to the box on the wall. She stopped and looked. She did not show surprise at once.

'I suppose the damn thing's right?' she said, staring at it.

As the wobbling became less the bell clanged again, and indicated the back door.

'It's not wrong,' she said slowly and very quietly. 'It begins to look as if we've been shopped.'

'What do you mean? How could somebody have found out — unless it was the murderer? He wouldn't play games like this.'

I took her arm.

'Show me to the loading bay. We must see who's at the back.'

She turned out of the passage through a big empty room, then into another. Neither was lit and the night-lights did not reach into the second room.

At the end of that room she pushed me towards an opening on my left. Through that I could see the grey concrete of a loading bay and the shadow of the handcart standing two steps down from my level.

The light from the sky itself came from a big opening on the left of the handcart. I pointed to that opening questioningly.

She breathed close to my ear, 'Yes.'

Very carefully I went down the two steps and crept along to the return of the front wall so that I could peer round the edge of the opening.

Cautiously I moved forward until I could see past the edge with one eye. I made out the part of a yard and the back wall and back door of the house on the left. Someone was standing close to the door, tapping a foot impatiently.

The light was not good, and the figure was unclear. I could not even see which way it faced, so I did not put my head out further.

The figure pushed the bell again, so I could make out which way it was facing, and pushed my head out a bit further to get a better look.

One thing at least I could make out when I looked with both eyes, and that was, it wasn't McGuffy working some trick with the electrics.

This figure was angry, fidgety. Not a bit like McGuffy, patiently tormenting, whether by making the landlord's ears scream or playing the bells both sides of the house at once.

This was a stockier, more restless person.

There was a sudden, lazy flicker of lightning far off. It stayed for a second, giving enough light for me to see the blonde hair, like blue glass strands, and the thrusting prow of Julie.

McGuffy at the front; Julie at the rear. At that moment it seemed this nocturnal visit was not to do with Helen Jane and her affairs, but to do with me.

They had both come for me.

I went back to the doorway where Helen Jane waited, and whispered what I had seen and what I thought.

She put a hand on my shoulder and pulled me inwards again. We went back into the first room.

'Why the hell would they come for you?' she whispered when it was safe to discuss it.

'I don't know why. But do you know her?'

'No. She's never been here, to my knowledge. I've done no business down there. I don't think my brother did, but I couldn't be sure of that. She couldn't have come for the other man, could she?'

'I don't know. But we can't get out while she's there.'

'Wait,' she said briefly, and went out to look for herself.

I followed her to the steps. In the quiet we heard Julie talking to herself.

'I'll make somebody hear! I'll make somebody bloody hear!'

It appeared that she then kept her finger on the bell and kicked the door till she hurt herself and stopped doing both. I went up behind Helen Jane when that happened and looked.

Julie seemed to be leaning a shoulder against the wall and holding her foot. She was also speaking rudely.

I thought hard for some way of getting her to go, but if I showed myself I felt that I knew what would happen.

About ten feet out from the door and towards us was a mounting stone. It had not seemed of importance until Julie started hopping towards it. She reached it and sat down to nurse the foot again.

Helen backed against me. We went back into the room.

'She's got to go before daybreak!' she said.

'Is there any other door we could get that cart to?'

'If there was I wouldn't be here now!'

'Then what the hell can we do?'

'There is only one thing,' she said. 'We can't shoot her. It would make a noise. And she might be killed. We'll have to take her from behind. Her back's turned.'

'Wait. We do that. It's not difficult. Agreed. But afterwards. What about afterwards? It would be hopeless. You know that.' I began to feel excited. 'Do you know what? You've lost your cool to suggest such a thing.'

81

She drew a long breath.

'Yes. I realise we couldn't possibly get away with it — unless it could be shown she was running away from the pub altogether.'

'How could that be shown?'

'Or I could go out, get her in, and give her something to ease the pain, and then we could go.'

'It's too wild. The only way is to wait till she goes.'

'But suppose she broke her toe?'

'For the lord's sake!' I was badly on edge then and glad of only one thing; that she was as bad as me. 'We shall have to put the whole thing off till tomorrow night.'

'We can't do that. If anything goes wrong with that wedding trip they'll all be back tomorrow.'

I felt there was something more than that sort of risk that made her so determined to get this business over and done with that night.

Maybe there was more behind the whole thing than I could see frankly, because I hadn't been prepared to see too far. My own interests had to overcome everything else.

I was determined to walk out of this job at the end of it without anything more than usual to worry about. It could be achieved and it might bring considerable rewards.

'If she's come up after you, what for? Let's get at it that way,' she said.

'I'm damned if I know. She wouldn't do it just for the roll. There must be something else.'

'What roll do you mean?'

'A roll in the hay,' I said impatiently. 'That's what she was after tonight. She wouldn't come up here for that. There must be something else.'

In the quiet after I had spoken I heard something rumbling.

'What's that?' I hissed to her. 'He's not sawing the door in, is he?'

'Don't be stupid — '

There was a short, startled scream from the woman outside. I almost ran back to the unloading opening to see what had happened.

It was raining. The storm had begun.

Julie was already on her feet and holding some sort of paper over her head. Swearing, she began to run with a limp, away from the house.

'She's going back,' said Helen Jane with a sigh of relief.

'With any luck, the rain'll drive that cigarette roller away as well,' I said. 'I'll go back and look.'

She started to come with me, but I began to run because I badly wanted to know whether he had gone or not. I had the feeling with him as of a millstone or albatross.

I went up the stairs and along to the brother's room once more. As I went in a lightning glare suddenly lit up the room brilliantly, then died within a second.

I stopped dead, close to the wall. The sound of heavy rain hissed on the stones outside after the fierce crack of thunder had echoed away down the sky.

A distant flare shed a flat grey light outside, and showed without any doubt that the curtains had been pulled back and the balcony outside was clear.

One thing which I notice as a matter of

course in strange houses is which side of the door the key is on, if there is one. At the brother's door it had been on the outside.

I backed along the wall, watching the darkness round me. It was useless to listen because of the noise of the rain.

The door came up against my back. I groped behind me for the handle, but I did not think that McGuffy would attack me. That did not seem to be his line at all.

Another lightning flash hit me in the eye while I was looking directly at the window. It left me with its shape picked out in greenish red on my sight as I opened the door and slipped back round it.

As I closed the door I automatically felt for the key. It wasn't there.

The storm was noisy at that time, the thunder crashing from nearby and also in the distance around. I looked up and down the corridor, which was empty.

McGuffy must be in the house somewhere. He alone could have taken the key from the corridor side of the door.

It was impossible to make up a reason for the curtains having been drawn back fully. The act seemed pointless, unless it was intended to let us know that he *was* inside.

First, why had he waited outside for so long if he had known the clear way in to start with?

I realised there was not much point in asking such questions of myself at that point. He was inside the house. That was the urgent matter.

The doors were all shut as I walked down the corridor looking for any sign there might have been of him hiding, but saw nothing.

The key had been removed so that we could not lock the door and cut off his way of escape. Perhaps then, his business was not with us, but with burglary.

But he had known that somebody was in the house that night and the persistent ringing of the bell must have been a try-on, to test if anyone was awake who would hear it.

It seemed easier to think that rather than that he had come to fix us.

When I came to the stairs she was nearly at the top.

'What's the matter?' she said, stopping quite still.

'He's inside,' I said.

'Are you sure?'

'Quite.'

The storm was moving away and the rain easing. For our problems the storm seemed to be at its height, and worsening.

5

She came up on to the landing and stood by me, looking along the corridor one way, then the other.

'The curtains are drawn, the windows wide open and the key's been taken from the door,' I said.

She said nothing but walked away towards the murder room. The sound of the rain far up on the roof had faded and there was only a sullen murmur of thunder in the far distance to show the storm was drifting away down the coast.

When she came to the door of the room she hesitated, then went in and closed the door quickly. I went up to it and stood there, listening as I kept watch on the empty corridor.

After a minute or more she came out again.

'He's gone,' she said. 'He was sheltering under the balcony. The rain's stopped. He just walked away down the drive.'

'He must have been in the room.'

'It seems so. But having got as far as the corridor, it looks as if courage failed him.'

'Or he'd seen as much as he wanted.'

She looked at me coolly.

'Yes. And he has gone at last, which just might indicate that he's got what he came for.'

'It couldn't have been a very secret need,' I said. 'He made such a din about it.' I turned towards the stairs. 'We had better get that box away.'

'Yes.'

My attitude to the box had changed since I'd found out McGuffy had been in the murder room. He could have seen nothing but that it was clean, and with no bedclothes, indicating that the usual occupier was away.

That, for him, must have linked with the fact that no one had answered the bell. He would have thought no one was in.

Any idea he might have had that I had come here could only have been a guess.

What Julie had wanted I had no idea. It

could not have been me, though I felt a slight annoyance at that, having believed all the evening that she had me in mind for that night.

Whatever had been behind the two visits, they had been at the house, and if that roused any outside suspicion of affairs that night, it was now important that there should be no corpse inside, just in case somebody turned up to have a look for the brother.

We went downstairs and along the bare passage. As we came in sight of the box I felt a queer sense of relief. As if it might have gone away on its own, or one of the nocturnal visitors had helped himself, like some anachronistic Burke or Hare.

As we lifted the box again my earlier feelings of nausea and horror of the contents were quite gone. The body had become a dead lump of dangerous matter that had to be got rid of quickly, and forgotten.

We carried it through the two store rooms and set it down on the wheeled funeral truck. That done she made a sign to me to stay where I was and went out to look round.

The clouds were breaking up, and patches of fitful moonlight came now and again. I watched her walk out of the yard, and after a minute or so, come back again.

'It's clear,' she said briefly.

I felt another spasm of relief. It was a spasm, for it came quickly and stopped abruptly as I took the rear handles of the cart.

The machine was silent. The rubber-tyred wheels thumped only faintly over the joins in the stone paving as we moved across the yard and out on to the gravel path down through the grounds.

The moon became bright, then died down into near darkness as it peered through rents in the mountainous clouds. I watched the light grey of her coat back as she moved between the front shafts of the cart.

We branched off the main path and into one between trees, which plopped heavy wet drops from their dying leaves above us. Once in amongst the trees the light became difficult, a mass of shifting shadows, sometimes lit, sometimes not. The grey shape of her back was about the only thing I could be sure of.

I think I saw something move towards her as we went quickly through the wood but my own sight was then cut off abruptly.

When taken entirely by surprise I don't think anyone can be quite sure of what is happening, but at the time I did think that a sack was thrown over my head, and I thought that because of the smell inside, and I react fast to smells that give me hay fever.

I tried to turn and hit out. I did hit something but then an arm was thrown round my throat and somebody grabbed my hands and began to rope them behind me. I kicked and hit the cart-wheel or a tree, which only hurt me.

No one spoke. Nothing was communicated by any hiss or grunt. I started to fall as my feet were swept from under me. A moment later something landed on top of me, something that struggled as much as I did.

The grass was wet on my hands tied behind me and I fought for breath inside the sack because the body of Helen Jane was lying on my face and her struggles made my situation worse.

Suddenly she stopped moving.

'Can you hear me?' she said, sounding muffled and faint.

I shouted, 'Yes!' and then started to sneeze.

She rolled off my face.

I bawled, 'Stay where you are! Don't move!'

Slowly I rolled so I was on my face and that brought me tight up against her back. I began to move upwards along the grass and felt my way up her back with my fingers.

When I felt the sack on her head I managed to get a hold of it and moved on again, pulling. It was a struggle. The sacking seemed to get caught under her chin, but it came off in the end.

'Okay. Sit up,' she said.

I heard her moving and then the sack was pulled slowly off my head. She did it with her teeth. When I could see, she was sitting on the grass with the sack lying in her lap.

The attackers had only tied our wrists, but they had done that pretty well. The moon came out again and we saw the cart lying on its side on the grass nearby.

'They've taken it!' she said in a strange, toneless voice.

'They thought it was guns,' I said, and sneezed. 'Are you quite sure that drugs was your brother's only interest?'

'I'm not sure of anything,' she said. 'How do you get up with no hands?'

'Get your back against a tree,' I said. 'Or you can do this.' I wriggled my legs till my feet came close up against me then leant forward and straightened slowly. I nearly fell on my face on the grass half-way up but steadied the overbalance with a shoulder against a tree trunk.

Once I was up I bent my knees, we locked fingers and I pulled her up back to back.

'A couple of bloody fools we look!' she said.

'Perhaps. But they were pretty considerate, taking everything into account.

They really believed we were going to hide a box of guns in the family tomb. Perhaps it has been done before.'

'And what will happen to my brother!' she demanded.

'They'll give him a burial,' I said. 'That's more than we were going to do.'

'You are cynical and callous,' she said with bitterness.

'For heaven's sake!' I protested. 'Get things into perspective.'

'Get back to the house!' she snapped very quietly. 'We must find something to cut these ropes. They're ruining my skin.'

We marched back to the house. I followed behind her. We only needed collars and chains to make a perfect column of chain gang convicts.

In the kitchen she got a table drawer open by pulling the handle behind her. There were plenty of knives in that drawer; the question was whether to use any of them.

The possibility was that a sharp knife would do more than ruin her skin or mine, it might cut a hand right off if used at the wrong angle.

The easy process used on film of using broken bottles, razor blades, carving knives or swords were easy to look at, but in practice almost impossible.

'Let's be civilised,' I said. 'I'll see what knot they used on you. It's safer than slashing your wrists. Turn round.'

She turned. I looked carefully at the turns and loops of the knot, a simple device whereby the knot gets tighter the more you try to pull it apart.

'Squeeze your hands tight together so the rope feels loose,' I said. 'Right. Now keep them like that.'

I did it with my teeth, and it took ten minutes with intervals for rest and when the first loop came undone the rest took ten seconds.

'You are clever,' she said, rubbing her wrists and looking at them carefully. 'I must get some cream.'

'You come back here and undo my bloody lot!' I shouted with great firmness.

She turned in surprise.

'I'm sorry,' she said and came back. She smacked my face. 'And don't shout at me.'

She cut my cords with one of the knives, which is easy when one's hands are not tied.

'Let's have a drink,' I said. 'Where is it? One always has drink after the burial to go with the funeral baked meats. I've had enough of attending the dead.'

She got some Scotch. We sat at the kitchen table.

'What will happen now, for the lord's sake?' she said, staring at me.

'Whoever those fellows were, they weren't legal,' I said. 'That was an arms raid. Instead of guns they've got a dead body. The only thing they can do about that is bury it quick.

'They don't want anything to lead to them and their business, whatever it is. They want guns. Obviously they've got some. They wanted more. They believed some were here, smuggled in by your brother. They took the wrong box, but they can't complain to anybody about that. You do understand their predicament?'

She stared right through me.

'Guns as well as drugs,' she said almost

97

to herself. 'That bastard's left me sitting on a powder barrel!'

★   ★   ★

'Not just you, Miss Wiseman,' I said. 'I'm sure that I'm now listed in Who's Who in the Crime Belt after that affair outside. It's bound to be thought I'm your partner.'

'I did tell you about the drugs, and the possibility of it bringing undesirable characters here. That was fair, I think,' she said. 'But I knew nothing whatever about guns.'

'You must have wondered where the box came from,' I said.

'I assumed it had been used to bring in dope. It did not occur to me he had been mixed up in arms, too.'

'How many would you guess ambushed us just now?'

'There were two on me. I know that.'

'I know the same. That's four. There may have been more. Putting one's head into a sack is a good gag, because you can't shout much and you can't hear much, either.'

'Did you hear a car go off?'

'No. But I'm sure one did.' I poured another drink for each of us. 'The point is, how did they know we were going to take the box down there?'

'They couldn't have done.'

'Unless your house is bugged,' I said. 'But if it was, they'd have heard that what we had in the box wasn't guns, so that's out. Then they must have been tipped off the box was there and that we would carry it down to the Tomb. How?'

I watched her.

'I don't know — Why are you looking at me like that?'

'You didn't tell them the box had guns in it, did you? It would have been an inspired way to get rid of a body.'

'It might also have turned me into a dead body, when they found out,' she said coldly.

'Let us take it from the beginning. Where did you find the box?'

'In the junk room at the end of the corridor upstairs.'

'It must have been brought here and

probably it was full of armour when it was. Where's that iron-work now?'

'I don't know. As I told you, it never occurred to me that it contained anything but drugs. These men might have thought it still did.'

'That's possible, of course. I feel in my bones they imagined guns, and when I was struggling I did feel a hard, heavy lump against my arm, far too heavy to be anything but metal and anything else but a pistol. A chain of thought, you see.'

'And I feel it's right,' she said.

'Now why did they jump us? Why didn't they wait till we put it in the tomb and then take it from there?'

'A good question. Why?'

'There must have been someone waiting *at* the tomb. Perhaps a car parked on the other side of the railing you spoke of.'

'Another lot!' she said, her voice was sharp in sound but curiously devoid of expression.

'There has to be a reason why they risked jumping us as they did when, if no one had been near the tomb, they could just have watched and waited.'

'I think you are right all along,' she said. 'While you were speaking I remembered something my brother said to me.

'I was very angry when I heard about the drugs. I said he would get himself mixed in with a lot of cut-throats and get himself killed.

'He made it very clear that contacts in the business were not that kind at all. It was a straightforward business between suppliers and distributors.'

'In the broad sense, he was right,' I said. 'It is a straight business and there isn't much violence amongst rivals. I don't know why it's so, I just know that up to now, it has been like that. Arms is different.'

'All right. You'd know that sort of thing, but the most worrying question is still unanswered.

'How did they know we would go down there with the box?'

'Shall we be logical?' I cocked my head at her.

'Of course.'

'Then the only possible answer is you

101

blew it to somebody.'

'What!' She jumped to her feet and looked as if she would kill me, but then cooled pretty quickly and sat down again. 'You were the only one I told.'

'Think again. When we first discussed these things, your servants were in the house.'

She looked at her drink and frowned.

'None of them came near us.'

'Somebody knew we'd take the box to the tomb tonight.'

'But why on earth should we — you and I — take a box of guns down there at night when it was thought outside that my brother was away?'

'Bear in mind that someone knows your brother is dead.'

'Yes.'

'That someone was in the house to kill him, and could have seen the box in the junkroom. Let's suppose it was full of guns then. Give him, theoretically, every assistance.'

'Yes. But he still wouldn't have known we would take the box down to the tomb.'

'Wait a moment. Someone got in

upstairs tonight. We had the box down in the passage. Suppose he was in the house when we were taking the box down and saw us?'

'Then he must have seen the walking hearse and guessed the connection. That is giving him too much, theoretically.'

'Then how? Julie at the back door. Let's say she saw the hearse. Then she had to see the man who had been in the house and they made two and two and passed on the word to the ambush gang, who had been waiting for two days for us to wheel the box to the tomb.'

'There is no sense in any of it,' she said shortly. 'They knew about the box and where we were taking it.'

'It would be a normal connection to think a hearse would be used in conjunction with a tomb, and the tomb is a ready-made hiding place few would suspect except those who have a special interest in finding hidden smugglings. And then — '

I stopped because I heard that soft ringing in my ear which makes us say that someone is thinking of us. It made me think of George.

And the bug stuck behind his ear.

A bug stuck on the box so that McGuffy could monitor just where it was going.

But if he had been doing that sort of secret work, what on earth was he doing ringing the bell for hours on end?

The answer to that must be that he hadn't had anything to do with a bugging of the arms box. More likely that had been done when the intruder had found the box the previous night, in the junk room.

If the intruder had been that slick, how had he been so amateurish and unsophisticated as to lose his temper and practically chop up a man in bed just afterwards?

It didn't fit.

But then nothing now seemed to fit. The woman and myself seemed to be the only two in the affair who had no clear idea of what we were doing.

I stood up.

'I'm going back. It'll be daylight in two hours.'

She looked up at me with a sulky sort of expression.

'No,' she said. 'You come to bed. I need soothing. I'm all edges.' She stood up.

'I said I'm going back,' I reminded her.

'Shut up and come to bed,' she said firmly.

'No!' I said, firmly.

'Yes!' she said, more firmly.

'Goodnight!' I said, and strode — I think — to the door.

'Wait!' she said. 'Look at me!'

I stopped. That old gag, I thought. I would turn and there she would be naked. But I had seen her naked, worked with her naked, we had sloshed about like naked car-women together. I turned slowly and with, I think, a slow smile.

But she wasn't naked. Not at all.

She had a pistol pointed straight at me, and as I watched, she flipped the safety catch with an elegant thumb.

'Get up the stairs,' she said.

She was holding it with both hands for steadiness, and for a moment I thought she might shoot.

Then I smiled and put on my hat — or nearly put it on.

'Goodnight,' I said, and as I raised it to my head, she fired.

It actually hit the hat and holed it right through. The shot went into a hanging advertisement calendar and lost itself in the plaster behind.

'I know now what the trouble is,' I said. 'You are off your head. Your cranium is swelled with illusions of invincible ego.'

I continued my criticism as I walked out and up the stairs in front of her.

At least, I thought, as I reached the bedroom door, the sable coat cannot say I erred of my own free will.

Helen Jane Wiseman was something of a woman.

'This is enforced dalliance,' I said as she closed the door.

'I'm sure it makes a change,' she said and threw the gun on the circular bed.

Curious, I picked it up and snapped out the magazine. It was full of bullets. I snapped it back and tossed the gun back on the bed.

'Where did you get that?' I said.

'I have come to relax, not discuss anything,' she said.

'I have had a bad night,' I said, undressing.

'You have made a muck of it so far,' she said, throwing her coat across the room. 'This is your chance to make good.'

★ ★ ★

It is always difficult to judge time in such circumstances and Helen Jane Wiseman was an extraordinary woman with very special gifts, which took my interest right away from my predicament.

In fact, after a while, I began to think in quite a new way: that I was in a mess one way and another, but now I had a staunch assistant.

Whatever the mess was, she would get me out of it. I would make sure of that.

Refreshed by this confidence in the future I continued to amuse her until we heard in the distance, the ringing of the bell in the passage by the kitchen.

'Let it ring,' she said.

But my mind was offtracked by the

interruption and another thought came into my head.

'Suppose,' I said, 'our ambushers were not after guns or drugs when they stole that box?'

'You're mad,' she said. 'What else could they want?'

She smiled.

'The body,' I said.

The smile froze.

'*What?*' she said.

6

At almost seven o'clock I came back into the alley beside the pub. I had seen one person, a postman beyond at the end of the alley, sitting on a bollard on the hard, waiting for something. He was smoking. I saw him against the glow of a lamp across the water on the horn of the harbour.

He made it necessary for me to make a silent climb.

I could reach the eaves of the shed roof at a point where there was a window with a wooden sill to provide foothold.

With both hands gripping the gutter I put a foot on the sill and lifted up and over the gutter on to the roof. The corrugated sections creaked slightly. I lay flat and looked down to the postman on the quay. He did not move.

It was quiet and still dark. I crawled across the roof to the house wall and came under the open leaves of my window. Once my fingers were on the sill, noise did not matter so much.

If the postman looked he would see nothing. I would be inside the room.

My action was fast, to make sure he would see nothing of me if he did look, though I don't think I made much noise in getting up and over the sill into the room.

There had been no lights on at the other windows of the pub, so I thought it best not to use any and began to undress by the faint glow from the window, which was growing paler by the minute.

I undressed slowly, because my head was full of the curious idea that the whole of the strange and bloody events of the night had been activated by someone's determination to get Wiseman's dead body.

The only reason I could think of for such a snatch was that the body wasn't Wiseman's at all.

If that were the case then Helen Jane must have organised the whole thing for some purpose of her own.

Thinking back carefully I could remember no family photographs in the big house. That is not unusual, for decorating the parlour walls with the faces of the fearful and familiar has rather gone out of fashion.

So that even if Wiseman's head had been unaffected by the murderer's battering, I should not have recognised him as H.J's brother.

Other people, however, would.

But if H.J. had organised any such thing, she could have done it without employing at least four people in an ambush, and further, there would have been no need at all to tell me anything about the murder, let alone get me involved as she had done.

As I have said, I was hampered all along by the fact that I believed she knew something about me which I did not wish to be publicised.

But perhaps my guilt had insisted on such a suspicion. She might have known nothing and really been in dire need of getting that murder cleared up and buried.

If that were the truth, and the body had been stolen for itself, what had been the bait there?

To hide a murder, which we were already doing, and about which activity they had had wind beforehand?

Or was there something on the body itself which was of value? A tattoo mark?

Or was it as we had at first thought; they believed the box to contain the guns that had originally come in it? Or otherwise, drugs?

Further events of that night must connect somewhere.

Had Julie passed on the word about the bier waiting and guessed it was there to carry the box they wanted?

Was McGuffy's continual ringing a ploy to keep us inside until he decided to go, by which time the ambush would have been laid?

That began to sound like the true connection.

I sat on the bed then jumped up quickly.

Somewhere in the room a bell began jangling. It started when I had sat down and went on a little after I'd got up.

I got a small torch from my coat

pocket, lifted the edge of the bedclothes and shone the beam underneath the bed.

A bell, still moving uneasily, had been hung by a hook under the springs. I reached under and unhooked it.

A joke perhaps. One of the worst jokes from my point of view, because it would prove to the joker that I had not gone to bed that night, if he had been listening for it.

I put the bell on the dressing table and laid on the bed to think. The window was growing brighter quite fast.

It was difficult to make up my mind whether the bell had been a sour joke by George, who had noticed more than we had given him credit for the previous night in the bar; or whether it had been put there to give notice of whether I used the bed or not.

Whichever it was I felt sure that either way, this damn pub was concerned with the shady business of Wiseman at the big house.

Suspecting that didn't help my thoughts. It made me feel more uneasy about my position than ever.

I tried to think clearly.

Julie had called at the house because she had something to do with Wiseman's business.

McGuffy had called because he was in the business of helping the ambushers steal Wiseman, or his assets.

By thinking that, at least I had got them separated.

There was a sudden knocking at the door.

'Do you want early morning tea?' Julie called.

'I'm already up,' I said. 'I'll come down for it.'

'Right. Same room as last night.'

I was tired, but my head was so full of animated rubbish floating about in all directions that I knew I should never sleep.

A radio was making its tinny noise out in the street, and drew away up the alley, fading so I could hear the sea again without realising I had been hearing it before.

It was getting restless. Perhaps a wind was rising with the coming day. I looked out of the front window at the curve of the little harbour in the grey light of dawn. Some lit windows of cottages on the other side looked like cold green lights.

The sea beyond the horns of the harbour was ruffled and here and there seamed with white streaks. The sky seemed low.

For a moment the scene looked like one of foreboding, and into my mind came a nightmare of the gun box drifting in from the sea, half submerged, and as it came into the calm water of the harbour red stains began to spread outwards from it.

I washed, dressed and went downstairs.

Half-way down I stopped and realised that I had opened my bedroom door without thinking of the bolt I had shot last night.

It had not been shot that morning.

My empty, tormented stomach tried to turn over and freeze inside me as I went on down. My legs felt weak and the weakness spread right through me so that, for a moment I no longer cared whether I ever got away from this entanglement or died in it.

Died was not too melodramatic. Wiseman was dead already, and I knew it, and others knew I knew it.

'There we are, dear,' Julie said, putting a cup of tea on the table. 'Sugar yourself, love. Going to be a wild day. Glass is down. Funny, after a storm, too. But you can never tell what the weather will do these days, can you? It's the satellites.'

I was glad of the tea. It restored my flagging spirits.

'Sleep all right?' she said, coming back.

'I don't think I moved all night,' I said.

She sat down after bringing herself a cup of tea.

'It's the change of air does that, you know. Makes you tired.' She leant on the table and her mighty bosom almost rolled out of her dress. 'Hungry? I'll tell you what's for breakfast.

'Bacon, local smoked. Old Burnham stuffs it up his chimney and has smouldering oak chips down below. Real stuff, and sausages! People come miles for Burnham's sausages. Superior as mad they are. Then tomatoes — Like an egg as well?

'George was a bloody nuisance last night. Didn't get to sleep till past four. Complaining about his head.'

'Did you find the thing behind his ear?'

'Oh yes. It was after that. Kept waking up and grabbing me and shouting. I wonder you didn't hear, he made such a row.'

'I suppose he hung a bell under my bed?' I said.

'A bell? What, the honeymoon bell? Well! of all the sauce!' She glared at the door to the stairs.

'It only rang on one side of the bed. I didn't notice it till this morning.'

'Oh well. Long as you can make allowances for softening of the brain — ' She got up. 'I'll start breakfast. Help yourself to more tea.'

I was then almost sure that I had made a mistake about Julie. Her behaviour was so normal, so lacking in any suggestion of deceit or guilt that I felt I must have made a mistake over the figure at the back door of the night.

The breakfast was superb. By the time I had had it, I had no doubt at all she was innocent of any kind of ulterior business.

When I was on to toast and her home-made marmalade, McGuffy came down the stairs, casual in his manner as during the night before.

'You ready for breakfast?' Julie said, coming into the room.

'No breakfast, thanks. Can't afford it. I'll just pay for the bed, thanks.'

'Well, I won't charge you much,' she said.

'No, thanks.'

'Have a cup of tea, then. I won't charge for that.'

He had that. He sat stirring it till she went out.

'Bloody row that George kicked up in the night,' he said. 'Must have been mad drunk.'

'Perhaps it was the pink elephant syndrome. When they come together with reality you get the screaming mimis.'

'Ah well, I must get walking. I'm going back to have another shot at that boathouse. The one in the creek. I'm damn' sure somebody's about there.'

'Hang on,' I said. 'I'll give you a lift. I haven't an appointment till later on.'

He sat down again.

'That's decent,' he said. 'Thanks.'

'Not a bit. I like to poke around the country when I can. Furthermore,' I lied, 'I've nothing else to do here till the appointed time.'

'Okay,' he said, and began to roll a cigarette.

★ ★ ★

He showed me the way. We went up the hill out of the town, along the top road for a distance alongside the Wiseman wall to the estate, and at the end, where I thought the tomb must be, we took a small turning left, marked 'Private Road — Dead End.'

It was very narrow and went fairly steeply down into a wooded valley which then broke out on one side to an open view of the river below.

We could see the boathouse building at the water's edge and the road stopped at

119

the back of it. Trees grew up the banks on either side of the creek and reached up to the top so that the boathouse was very secluded.

The trees, however, could also have hidden an army of spies without showing any sign of activity. The slopes of the valley were red with falling leaves and the golden trees were thinning as they shed their dress.

'There's no car here,' I said as we stopped. 'In fact, it looks deserted.'

'I'll have a look. I'm sure somebody comes here.'

'But didn't the woman at the house tell you whether there is a man here or not?'

'She didn't seem to know a lot about it. Said it was her brother's. He was keen on boats.'

He was eyeing the big wooden building as he spoke, and I think he spoke carelessly.

'He *was* keen?' I said. 'Is he dead?'

He looked at me.

'I'm talking like 'she said he was keen on boats',' he explained sharply. 'I don't

120

know anything about him, dead or alive.'

'Oh, I see. It's a big place,' I said, and went to a window.

It was dirty but I could see through the glass to a water-filled dock inside the building. There was a small motor yacht in it, and two or three other boats were lying about on the floor on stocks.

McGuffy walked off by the wall, looking in one small window after another. I followed him casually round the end of the building and down the bank to the entrance door to what looked like the office.

He tried the handle. He tried it hard, then he bent and examined the lock.

'Well, this is used every day,' he said. 'You can tell that by the handle.' He stood back a pace and looked up at the gable end of the building.

'What are you really after, McGuffy?' I said.

He looked at me, his greeny-grey eyes very small and sharp.

'What do you mean?' he said.

'To hell with it!' I said, and said it sharply, even angrily. 'You are here for a job. You're looking over the place for a break-in!'

He was silent a moment, as if taken aback, then eased off and shrugged.

'To steal what? I've got all the tools I want.'

'Tools?' I made it sound scornful. 'I'm not talking about tools! I'm talking about the proceeds of smuggling.'

That shook him, and I could see it did in one short moment of alarm in his face. The moment was lost very quickly.

'Smuggling?' he said, showing no emotion after the initial shock. 'Who the hell are you?'

'I think you already know who I am, but not what my work here is.'

'You're some sort of eye. I guessed that. So you've got to be looking for something.'

'I am here to trace some papers for the family up at Ravenleigh. Now tell me what you're here for?'

He stared.

'Oh you think I've got them? These papers? Or do you think I've come to pinch 'em?'

'I said, tell me what you're here for.'

'I've told you all that.' He began to look very angry. 'Just hold on a minute, anyway. I've no duty to tell you anything.'

'Right. I'll tell you what your interest here is.'

He went very still. I was watchful in case he decided to make some kind of assault on my person, if not existence.

He did nothing, but stayed standing close to the door in a weird, rigid sort of way.

'There is someone inside here,' he said, very quietly. 'I had an idea there was somebody round-about.'

I watched him, not the door he looked at. He was very tense as he stood looking at the panels as if willing his eyes to see right through.

He needn't have bothered to make contact because I was sure anybody inside could see him, probably through the window beside the door.

'I have to go now,' I said. 'You might as well wait around. Somebody may come down here later.'

He looked at me then.

'Yes,' he said. 'Thanks for the lift. I'll hang around on the offchance. I want the job, you see.'

The conversation was designed to make anyone inside less suspicious.

I turned and went to the corner of the building, then looked back.

What I saw astonished me, and changed my mind about him being an undercover man either for law or disorder.

The silly sod had drawn back a few paces and even as I watched he ran at the door and charged it with all his weight.

There was a crash, then a cracking of splintering wood, then some more cracks and bangs as if he had got inside and was falling on, or knocking over, furniture.

As the noise of assault died down I remained there at the corner looking towards the doorway. If anyone had been inside I should have heard further noises, but heard only the soft running of the water between the piles of the boathouse landing stage.

He had probably knocked himself out, I thought and moved back towards the door. I stopped and listened and still heard nothing but the water.

The fact of the matter was that I felt as keen as he had to see inside Wiseman's boathouse, and as he had conveniently made way for me, I went to the doorway.

Still there was no sign of activity. I leaned forward and looked in the doorway.

The charge had flung the door flat down on the floor inside an office with a sloping desk by a window and a lot of dirty, neglected looking papers piled around anyhow. There were files on wall shelves, a couple of tables with more papers on them, and three wooden stools scattered round.

There was no McGuffy but there was some blood on the prostrate door, so he had not got away without hurt.

There was an open door on the far side of the little room leading on to a wooden gallery overlooking the boat shop below.

I made very sure that there was nobody hiding behind the desk or one of the tables and then went through on to the gallery.

It was a sizeable workshop, and signs of extensive repairing work lay on the shop floor below.

Another thing that lay on the floor below was McGuffy.

He lay on his face, quite still.

There was no sign of anyone else below.

I backed into the office again and again made sure no one was there, for after all, the place had no door. The door lay as before, flat down facing its opening, as if both top and bottom hinges had burst together at the same time.

The bloodstains were at about chest height.

At first I had thought McGuffy must have hit his nose and bled at once, but it was too low and not that kind of splash stain.

Rather it looked as if he had been bleeding from the front, lower down, as if from a wound. It could be a wound that came, as the door fell a fraction in front of him, from a shot fired as soon as he had flashed into view.

There had been noise enough to hide

the report which would have come at almost the same time as the rest of the crashing noises.

I went out, back to my car and drove away from that place.

* * *

When I pulled up outside the main terrace at Ravenleigh I took a good look at the balcony outside Wiseman's bedroom before I rang the bell.

There was a fair amount of creeper up the wall at the front of the house so that the climb to the balcony presented no problem except the making of rustling noises on the way up.

H.J. opened the door, as expected.

I said, 'Before we talk of other things; I've just come from looking at your boathouse down on the creek. What goes on down there?'

She shrugged.

'I don't know. It might have been used for his smuggling but I doubt it. Surely that would have been very foolish?'

'There was somebody in there — in the

building just now.'

'Who?'

'I didn't see them. I just know somebody was there.'

'As I say, I don't know what went on down there. It was my brother's, absolutely. And further, I've no real interest in boats, except large ones with luxury suites.'

'I thought we might look at the wood where the ambush was. Get the cart back,' I said.

'I'll get a coat.'

The wind was getting blustery when we walked down the gravel drive towards the trees. Near the beginning of the wood we turned off to where we had been ambushed the previous night.

The handcart was still there on its side but there was no other sign of the incident lying around. She stood watching me look over the ground around the spot.

'Well?' she said, as I stopped.

'Nothing but kicked up grass here and there. I can't see anything that's been dropped. I wonder what your brother was really up to? Drugs, he said. Now that it seems like arms as well, I begin to wonder if he had an interest in any particular revolutionary party of any particular country.'

'I've been wondering that since last night.'

'And having wondered did you remember anything which might have fitted in with such an idea? Any small detail of what he did recently, or what his callers were like.'

'You don't think I haven't tried already?' she said angrily. 'No. I can't think of anything that could help.'

I turned and looked away through the wood.

'I want to see inside the tomb,' I said.

She looked surprised and angry.

'What!' she said.

'Inside the tomb,' I said. 'Suppose the box was put in there when it was found what was inside?'

7

'I haven't got the key of the tomb,' Helen Jane said, firmly.

'Then go back and get it,' I said. 'I'm in this far enough. I want to know now where I stand. What's likely to fall on me. I want to see in the tomb.'

'You can fetch the key,' she said. 'In the library. The drawer in the big table. You can't mistake the key.'

I turned to go when she spoke.

'Did you see that man who called? The one you said was at the pub?'

'Why ask that now?' I said curiously.

'I don't know, but just standing here it suddenly felt like last night. As if somebody was watching.'

'Well, *he* isn't watching,' I said. 'He's dead.'

She started. Her eyes opened pretty wide.

'Where? Down there? How?'

'In your brother's boathouse. Shot.'

I turned and went off, walking quickly to leave her to stew over the news and the questions she would want to ask.

The big key was in the drawer as indicated. As I closed the drawer again I looked up and through one of the main windows overlooking the front drive.

There was a car pulled to one side of the road just outside the gates. I could see no one in it.

The road went nowhere but to the house drive. The woods out there were commonland, I supposed. From the eminence of the window I could see over Ravenleigh's walls and a good distance into the wood, but saw no people at all.

Of course, anyone could park there and go for a long walk. The only thing was that but for the elevated position of the windows, I shouldn't have seen the car at all.

I took the key and went back to where she waited by the trees and the toppled hearse. As soon as I got to her she started to talk.

How did I know about McGuffy? Had I been down there? Why?

I just said, 'After we've been in the tomb. Come along.'

We went through the wood and joined a fairly wide path which led from the main drive further over, straight to the tomb.

It was a great stone block of Victorian splendour, darkened by weather and stained by the drips from the trees which almost covered it against the sky.

The Ravenleigh wall continued behind the tomb and curved round it so that it was mainly kept private from the road outside. About ten yards to the right the wall broke down into a lower barrier, about four feet high with railings on top. This ran as far as an iron gate, which stood as high as the top of the railings, and then, further on the wall continued as high as the main one. The railed part was for the public to watch the funeral, perhaps.

Not over-keen to open the tomb, I went over to the iron gate. It was locked and further, there was a chain and padlock, also locked.

She watched me.

'It hasn't been forced, has it?'

'Why should it be? One could get over the main wall with an acrobatic scramble. That is, after throwing a sack across all that ancient broken glass on top.'

I went to the tomb. There were steps down to what looked like a heavy bronze door.

'I should think this cost as much as a small house,' I said.

She came up behind me.

'Hold it,' she whispered in my ear. 'There's someone on the other side of the wall.'

I stopped and looked round. She stepped to one side. From where I stood just down the steps I could see the sun throw a slanting shadow down the first four railings nearest us. It moved very slightly as I watched.

I was glad I had not encouraged any questions about McGuffy while we were near that wall. I was in trouble enough already, and if any unfriendly person overheard the fact that I had been the man to go down to the boathouse with McGuffy, they might think I had had a direct hand in his demise.

Come to think of it, I even had a motive, it would appear to an outsider.

The problem for us at that moment was just what to do about someone being on the outside of the wall. It was the side of the public road out there and we couldn't stop anyone standing on it.

The best thing seemed to be to act it out.

'It's very handsome,' I said, doing a bit of a mime for her. 'I shouldn't have thought the weather would have got through that lot on top.'

'It's a bit cracked up there,' she said, catching on. 'I am worried about it. You would know what's best to do about it.'

The shadow on the railings moved slightly, but that was all.

'It might be easier,' I said, 'if I got on top and had a look. Do you mind?'

'Whatever you think best,' she said.

The deep carved mouldings and panels in the stone made it easy to climb because, at the back of the tomb, the ground had not been cut away to let people down to the level of the vault floor.

I got on to the flat top of the stone hulk where the branches of a tree growing close to the wall almost touched one edge of the roof.

My companion kept up a pretty vocal line in anxiety for my safety while I edged along the tree branch to the trunk, where, by leaning over, I could see down the other side of the wall.

Down below a man stood in the faded blue of denim. He was wire-haired. He had his hands in the front pockets of his trousers. As I watched, he took them out and began to roll a cigarette.

Fascinated I studied the jacket and the canvas bag over his shoulder and everything was exactly McGuffy, except that I could not see the face.

I even recognised certain stains on the shoulder which had been on my side when we had driven down to the boathouse.

Very quietly I returned to the tomb roof.

'I can't see any cracks up here,' I said.

'But we'll take a look inside as well, just to make sure.'

'I wouldn't worry myself, quite honestly,' she said loudly, 'but it is a condition of my father's will that we have it inspected every two years.'

'I understand,' I said, and descended.

When I went round the grass to her she looked askance, but I made a scrub-out sign with my finger and she nodded.

We went down the little steps to the tomb door. I took the big key from my pocket and pushed it into the keyhole.

The push was enough to start the door moving silently inwards. I heard her draw a sudden sharp breath behind me, as I helped the slow-moving door with the flat of my hand.

An angled shaft of daylight hit the floor and its reflection did not do much to relieve the utter darkness inside that silent place.

My eye caught a gleam of something bright on the wall by the doorway close to me. Looking closer I saw it was an electric lantern hanging there.

'Can you see?' she said.

'There's a lantern here.' I unhooked it and flicked the switch on the back. The battery had been left almost too long. The light that shone out was poor, but in that gloom, almost enough.

There were two lines of slate shelves and four coffins standing on them. The brass handles were dull and the wood dark. They stood on the shelves facing the door but there were others and as I turned to look on them the lantern battery gave up the ghost.

'Four coffins,' I said. 'Is that about right?'

'I suppose so. Yes, I think it would be. Let me look — '

I pushed her back.

'Stand in the door,' I said. 'Make sure it stays open.'

'Nerves,' she said, very quietly.

My nerves were not that bad, but if we got shut in this tomb it would be far too late when anybody got us out.

'The door was unlocked,' I said, and brought my small torch from my pocket. It was almost too small to be of much use owing to the contrasting shadows made by the brilliant patch of sunlight on the floor.

'Nobody took the key,' she said, keeping her voice low. 'I'm sure of that.'

'I think somebody picked the lock and couldn't — or didn't have time — to lock it again,' I said. 'The shelves here have been used. The slate's scratched. Something was here. Something heavy. Not coffins. Otherwise there's nothing else but legitimate occupants. Let's go.'

We went out. She locked the door.

The shadow had gone from the railings when we started our walk back to the house. On the way I righted the hearse and pushed that up with us.

*   *   *

We went into the library. She put away the vault key. I looked out of the window. The car was still there.

'Who was it waiting by the wall?' she said.

'It looked like McGuffy, but McGuffy's dead.' I told her as much as I knew about it. 'I think the man by the wall had his clothes, which must mean the body's been disposed of already.'

'That sounds professional, doesn't it?'

'Much too professional. He went where he wasn't wanted and — click! — dead and gone at a stroke and his cover used by somebody else.'

'What do you mean — cover?'

'I think he was an agent for somebody. He was investigating, no doubt of that. He had no compunction about busting the door in when he felt he had to get in.

'It was unlucky somebody was in there, that's all.'

'They didn't shoot you when you went in.'

'No. McGuffy must have been something special, or he knew something he didn't tell anybody about. He must have been very special, come to think, since his shoes are being filled straightaway.'

I sat down.

'I'll take a drink,' I said. 'My knees are beginning to weaken. There is a nasty feeling coming over me that you have led me into a fight with Goliath. I'm not the type. I'm a poor shot with a sling.'

'Well, I didn't suspect anything like this!' she said, angrily. 'I'm sorry, too! I've read about concrete boots.'

She got some Scotch and poured. We sat for a while on opposite sides of the table, sipping Scotch and trying to think of ways out of the mess.

'I only came here to find a will,' I said. 'Now look at it all! Two murders, dope running, gun running — everybody's running but us, and we're the ones who ought to run.'

'I stay here, whatever happens.'

'And I go — I hope,' I said. 'But I don't want to go with the feeling that there is a canful of red hot thugs, dope gangs and arms racketeers tied to my tail. I suppose it sounds ridiculous, put like that, but it's a fact.

'Your brother was more than a tycoon. He was Pandora in drag.'

'My brother wasn't killed in a fit of temper,' she said.

'I'm glad you've realised that,' I said. 'I'm sure now he was killed by the same lot as killed McGuffy and for some connecting reason. Let's say McGuffy

140

was investigating the tentacles of your brother's drug business.'

'That sounds right. I suppose if he investigated he would reach a point where he would realise who needed my brother dead.'

'Yes. Now who? What is it really to do with? Arms and drugs have two entirely different kinds of villains around them. I'd say arms has the rougher.'

'I'd no idea about arms,' she said.

'We might get a lot of help once your staff gets back,' I said. 'They're bound to have noticed things that you may never have seen. Servants always do.'

'Perhaps. They may have seen callers I didn't. But did he have that kind of caller? I don't think he would have done. He had the boathouse. He had other landing places. He needn't have even seen the stuff that came in.'

'He probably didn't, as you say. He wasn't a distributor. Okay. Assume the drugs never came near this house. But the arms did.'

'Well, the box was here,' she said.

'But he would hardly have brought an

incriminating box here if it hadn't come here in the first place. And heavy boxes were stored in the tomb. The scratches give it away, and the door lock was picked.'

'Yes, that may be so. But if they knew the boxes were in the tomb why ambush us last night?'

'I can't get rid of this illogical idea that they wanted your brother's body.'

'To destroy the evidence against them?'

'We were doing that for them. I'm sure they knew that.' I sat back and stared hard at her. 'You'd thought all this out, maybe in a hurry, but you must have decided what to tell your staff. After all, your brother wasn't going to show up any more.'

'I should have told them we had a big row and broke up for good. They knew we'd had a lot of rows recently. One of them was the reason why he lost his temper and hit me with the drug business. They'd have swallowed that.'

I moved to one side then so she could see the middle window.

'There's a car outside, just past the

gates. It's been there some time. Does it look familiar?'

She got up and looked hard.

'It looks like Cook's car!' she said.

'Does it?' I said. 'Then perhaps we'd better go and see if it is.'

'Yes. I think we should.'

Once again we went out, this time across the terrace and down to the drive. She walked fast. There was something odd about her manner, as if she'd lost the fear I'd seen showing in the last hours and was now very angry indeed.

When we came to the car she looked in. It was empty. No one was on the floor. She opened the door.

'The keys are still in,' she said, straightening. 'What on earth did she leave it out here for? She always takes it round the back of the house. This is very odd.'

I went round to the back and tried to lift the boot lid. It was locked.

'Bring the keys,' I said.

She brought them round. There were a number of keys on the ring, obvious house keys and others but there was no key that fitted the boot lock.

'Drive it in to its usual spot behind the house,' I said. 'And put your gloves on.'

'I haven't any in this coat.'

I had. I drove the car. She walked behind and in the mirror I could see she was angrily thoughtful. When I turned to go round the house she was walking fast towards the terrace.

At the back yard I stopped and got out and tried to surprise the lock with sudden jerks. But it was an old car like they don't build any more, and the lock held fast.

I got into the rear and tried to pull the backs of the seats forward so I could see into the boot. That was difficult too.

By the time I'd got it loose at one corner, Helen Jane was standing by, watching. I could see a little part of the boot by holding the seat pulled out as far as I could at that corner. Once again I got out my torch and shone it down the narrow gap behind the seat.

I let it go again and put the torch back in my pocket.

'Is there anything there?' she said.

'A woman. I should think it's the cook.'

She just stood there staring at me.

'Good God!' she said. 'Where's this going to end? Why kill her?' She turned and paced up and down for a minute or more, then stopped. 'How did the others go without her?'

'I'm beginning to wonder if the others did go. Something blew wide open in this place yesterday and it blew up everybody involved. And Cook must have been in it. Bang goes your jolly alibi or whatever you call it. But what about the others?'

'They couldn't all have been in this drug business!' she said.

'Look, when somebody finds out what's going on, the person who is discovered has got to do something for protection. He can pay for silence or shoot for the same return. I should imagine your brother paid then the people who killed him started to sort out his partners.'

'This is slaughter!' she said, very quietly. 'What the hell can we do now?'

'Well, we've gone too far to call the police. We'd be in the clink before they started looking for anybody else.'

'But when the others get back — ' She looked at me. 'Well, they can't all be dead. They must have gone and didn't wait for Cook. Perhaps she said she'd follow. She was a very independent woman.'

'It's no good guessing what they did. If they're all right they'll come back as expected. If they're not, they won't.

'As far as we're concerned we know that three murders have been committed. One body — probably two — has gone, we don't know where. What was intended for this one, I don't know. I think they meant to come back for it.'

'Why do you think that?' she said sharply.

'There's no key to the boot but they've got one.'

'Another key,' she said. 'A key to the tomb, now this one.'

'If that's a link it's too faint to be worth thinking about.'

'Is it? But supposing they have a key to the house as well?'

'I thought you said the chauffeur

146

locked up at night? Surely he shoots the bolts?'

'Yes. I believe he does. It was just an idea.' She began to pace again. 'But Cook! I can't understand it.'

I took her arm, firmly.

'Let's go indoors. I want to talk to you.'

She looked at me in surprise. I pushed slightly on her arm and she went towards the house door. We went back into the library.

'Sit down, Miss Wiseman,' I said.

She looked surprised, but she sat.

'What's the matter with you?' she said. 'Haven't we enough trouble without histrionics?'

'Listen to me and don't talk until I've finished,' I said. 'First, I was invited here to find a missing will. I believe that was so originally. Further events prevented me doing anything about it.

'Because as soon as I got here you told me about your brother and asked my help. You gave the reason that you wanted to defend the family name, which I accepted.

'I did so because I have come across

that sort of pride before, professionally, and on two occasions it was genuine.

'But in all three cases I had there was also the consideration that if the family name began to smell, there would be some financial loss. In fact, it always seems that there might be some material loss in these cases.'

'What's this to do with my case?' she said angrily. 'My father is long dead. My brother's business is nothing to do with me materially. I have assured you of that.'

'But you haven't assured me that you have no business interests,' I said. 'Some sort of business which can be successfully operated from here, by someone with a car as agent.'

'You are thinking of Cook?'

'Yes.'

'What sort of business do you imagine I would operate from the middle of nowhere like this place?'

'Guessing isn't really my business. Where did you get that pistol?'

'I've had it for years.'

'Always fully loaded?'

'What's the good of one that isn't? If

you get a violent break-in at a lonely house like this, it's best not to wait to be assaulted, tied up or murdered.'

'Why didn't your brother think of that?'

'That's a bit of a cold one, isn't it?'

'It's all cold in this place. Cold and calculating. Your fear was not for the family honour, but for your business interest, which isn't above board.'

'I thought you didn't guess?' She was very cool.

'I'm not guessing when I say that you lied about that gun. You haven't had it for years, because that gun has small modifications which the manufacturers did not introduce until last year.'

'So?'

'Are you in the arms business?'

'And let myself be ambushed?'

'No. To fool the ambushers. They'd think the box was full of guns as usual, but in fact it got rid of an inconvenient body.'

She got up then and walked to the window and back.

'Well, if I have some business on the side, I naturally want to keep it quiet.

149

That is why I hired you, because you, too, have some business to keep confidential.'

So she did know that. It was almost a relief when she brought it out. At least I didn't have to wonder any more.

'Fraud, I understand,' she said. 'Of course, unintentional. Everything was to be paid back before anyone noticed, but — oh dear! — nothing came back, did it?'

'Not enough,' I said. 'But it *was* managed, with skill and a bit more time, though as you say, the crime remains. Like yours.

'On top of everything else, Miss Wiseman, Cook is now dead out there. And the man who kept calling here is dead down at the creek. What next, I wonder?'

She looked at me and smiled. I shook my head and smiled back.

8

We sat each side of the big table, looking at each other. The loose elegance which gave her an unusual beauty also added to the impression she gave of silently fighting me and winning.

'I see,' I said. 'So we now have a locked position of mutual blackmail.'

She shrugged.

'If you want to put it that way,' she said casually. 'But, as you say, such a position is locked so neither of us can move without suffering; the sensible thing, then, is to start again and talk of the best solution which will benefit both of us.'

'We can't do that without full knowledge of what the situation really is,' I said. 'So far, I've been playing this game with half the scene blanked off. Best start afresh by telling me what your private business really is.'

'I have no need to make money by dangerous investments.'

'You seem quite used to dangerous situations.'

'You mistake determination for experience.'

'How did you find out about my predicament?' She smiled.

'My father was one of the syndicate which you defrauded. Only he knew of the loss and allowed time for you to cover up.'

I felt easier instead of more tense.

'So?' I said. 'He knew and did nothing? So he too was straying on to the shadier side of the financial street.'

'A fair guess. It was a case of opposing rogues having to pause to protect themselves.'

'As now,' I said. 'So you waited until the day you needed help that couldn't be withheld and then called me.'

She smiled again.

'You forget,' she said, 'I called you some time before you finally came. You weren't well, you said. Remember?'

'That is true. I am thinking of a way to get over that difficulty.' I sat back. 'However, now we are putting our cards down — did you kill your brother?'

'No.'

'I ask because although I think there was a professional motive behind the killing, it was carried out by an amateur. I am still tied down by the absence of the rest of the staff. They would know all kinds of useful things.'

'You know when they're due. I can't bring that time forward.'

'Let's get back to the dead woman,' I said. 'She came every day. From where?'

'Just beyond the village. A cottage down on the beach round the headland.'

'Is she any relation to the woman at the inn?'

'She has a sister down there who works in the village. It might be at the pub. I don't know.'

'I was thinking that it could have been the reason for the barmaid coming up here last night, perhaps worried that her sister hadn't been seen.'

'Possible.'

'What does Cook look like? I couldn't make out just now.'

'Outsize. Not tall, but traditional comic

cook shape. Pretty in a way,' she said, watching me steadily. 'But why should the sister — presuming it is — come up here at midnight or after because her sister hadn't been home? She wasn't due to be home. She was supposed to go to the wedding.'

'She might have planned to go this morning.'

'Yes. She could have made it, but I understood she would follow the others when they went.'

'It would appear she said she would be back for something last evening, and when she didn't come, the sister came to find her.'

'As good a guess as any.'

But there was the fact that Julie's behaviour that morning had seemed too ordinary to have allowed for hiding the signs of wandering half the night in a storm. Further she had said George had been restless all night and he would have been able to bear that out, had I asked him.

'It's something that can be followed up,' I said. 'Now to the guns.'

'And what are they to do with me?' she said.

'Tell me.'

'I knew guns had come into the house after I had been told of the drug running.'

'Were you told about guns?'

'No. I came upon a box. Hand weapons. Italian, although the box was unmarked. It was in the attic amongst some old rubbish up there. The box hadn't been there long. There was no dust on it.'

'When was that?'

'Four days ago.'

'Did you ask your brother about it?'

'I accused him. He said there were no proper guns up there. He took me up there to look. The box was there. When he opened it it had only old flintlock pistols and other ironware he said he'd picked up at a sale.'

'So he knew you'd been looking.'

'Before I mentioned it. Yes, obviously.'

'What did you do about it?'

'I did nothing.' She leaned her hands on the table. 'The situation between my brother and I had become somewhat more than tense. I had been shattered by the drug confession. Guns as well — or the possibility — became too much. We just rowed if we met so we tried not to meet. It got very bad. I'm afraid that will be most of what the staff will have to tell you.'

'They would have been bad witnesses for you in your brother's murder.'

'Too bad. I have been playing a game of defending myself more than the family reputation.'

'That's the normal situation,' I said. 'But it's the only normal thing there is in this business. Have you found a sword?'

'I haven't found anything bloody or recently cleaned. I supposed that was what I should look for.'

'Nothing up there that is regularly cleaned, so that additional cleaning wouldn't be noticed?'

'I can't think of anything.'

'There is more than the servants' talk of your bad relations with your brother,' I said. 'That was his position. It was clear that he was lying in bed, or sitting up, rather — and talking to the person, I would say.

'Then suddenly he realised what was going to happen and he started to get up to reach the end of the bed. That is the curious movement.'

She watched me with a glint in her sharp eyes.

'We spend half our lives in bed,' I went on, 'and we get out of it on one side or the other. Unless something alarming happens, it would never occur to get out over the footboard. The clothes would be a hindrance.'

'Go on.'

'The signs point to him sitting there and talking to someone standing at the foot of the bed. Suddenly he saw the person produce a weapon. He tried to get at it in the quickest way, instead of getting out of the way of it, on either side of the bed.

'This seems to indicate he knew the person well enough to think he could persuade them out of using the weapon, rather than thinking that they would use it.'

She sat back.

'That's clever,' she said slowly. 'Some-one he knew well.'

'Someone he wasn't surprised to be talking to from the foot of the bed. Someone who would not rouse his curiosity by walking past the bed and into the deeper part of the room.'

'One of the staff!' she said.

'Or you, of course.'

'Yes. I exclude myself because I have knowledge which you haven't. I know I didn't kill him.'

'Things are beginning to get clearer, at least in some departments,' I said. 'One of the staff murdered him. Let's say Cook, who could use a cleaver and wash it without anyone taking notice.

'And now Cook is dead. So if the motive was professional, then she was put up to doing murder and afterwards kept quiet.'

'What about the man you say died down at the boathouse?'

'He came to find out something, I think, but I also have that idea of him ringing the doorbell to hold up our funeral procession till the ambush was ready.'

'If so, what was the ambush for?' she said. 'To get guns or get evidence?'

'Nobody would go to that length to get evidence. An investigator could just call and start collecting it, specially if he suspected guns were already in the building.'

'I suppose so. So whichever way you look, from my brother's murder to Cook's and on to the McGuffy man, there is a gang and it's right here.'

'Yes.'

She looked very straight then.

'So we don't stand a lot of chance of survival, do you think?'

'My hope is that there are two gangs,' I said. 'One against the other.'

'Could there be?'

'There are two separate items in demand; guns and drugs. There is money in each or more money in both together. Big illegal business, in which the gangs probably don't think you and I really have a part.'

'In any case, if we had a part, we

haven't the strength to oppose gangs.'

'Exactly,' I said. 'And would we oppose? If a gang organised your brother's death, they would also know we tried to hide the evidence of it.'

'So we couldn't talk?' She smiled. 'Blackmail again.'

'Which is where we came in,' I said.

She smiled slowly.

'There are possible lines of communication though,' she suggested.

'Quite a few,' I agreed. 'There are Julie and George at the pub and your staff. Questioning here could turn up a good penny.'

'But isn't it dangerous now to keep on probing if gangs are at the back of everything?'

'Miss Wiseman, there is one time, and only one, when one may walk out of danger with confidence, and that's when the danger has been defused.

'I was told there are three ways to treat a tiger. Make friends with it, try and kill it, or convince it that if it follows you, you will kill it. The last is the best. Friendship is uncertain. Trying to kill it can come to grief. Persuasion takes intelligence of all the relevant kinds.'

'I'm no philosopher,' she said. 'Nor are you, but you have experience, so I will follow you.'

★   ★   ★

'Some air has been cleared,' she said. 'But clouds remain. What about the man who took McGuffy's clothes?'

'I think he'll turn up,' I said. 'He had a purpose in taking the clothes and in standing down by the tomb. We have to wait, now; first for him, second for someone to come for Cook's car — if they don't fuse into the same person. Third, the return of the staff.'

'What could *they* know now?' she said.

'Cook couldn't have been mixed up in some important business without the others noticing something out of the way.'

'Surely I would have heard, too?'

'Not if they were all in it.'

She got up. She looked angry again, after a long time of being agreeable.

'I should have heard about it! They

couldn't all cheat me!'

She walked to the door and opened it.

'I'll get some food,' she said.

I got up.

'No. We'll go down to the pub and eat. We might hear something there.'

'I thought we were waiting here?'

'The only people likely to arrive in daylight are your servants. They won't go again.'

She agreed as if she didn't care much one way or the other. I drove her down and parked on the hard.

There were several men in the bar. One or two looked round at us and then two more did, as if they'd been nudged. Julie paused in serving and stared curiously.

Helen Jane sat in a pew. I ordered drinks and asked about lunch.

'There's some fish just in,' she said. 'I'll tell you what it is — or come and choose your own. That'll be better.'

I followed her out into the kitchen. There was a flat basket of fish there.

'Nice young ray there,' she said. 'I could poach that in some wine for you. Ray, black butter. Very light, very

162

pleasant, seeing as you've got a rather special woman with you.'

'We are merely doing a little business,' I said. 'Her servants are away at a wedding.'

'Oh, yes. Me sister was going up there, too, but she didn't. Last minute change. She's like that. Always having Last Minutes. Can't make her bloody mind up, that's the truth of it.'

'I'm surprised she missed a wedding. I thought women enjoyed them.' I laughed. 'It must have been very important, whatever it was.'

She came close and spoke low.

'I'll let you into a little secret; she has a little side business buying the food for up there. She's got a wholesaler who supplies Supermarkets. She gets a good cut. Local man, too, he is, so it's handy.'

'And she had to see him instead of going to a wedding?'

'Something cropped up, she said. Perhaps he got found out!' she laughed and opened the garden door. 'George! come in and take the bar. I've got to cook!' She slammed the door again. 'Has quite a few sidelines, my sister. You know, agency for these big warehouses? Wonderful catalogues.'

'Got quite a few contacts, then?' I felt excited but tried to look no more than pleasantly interested, though I also felt a slight shame at leaving my guest so long.

'Yes. I'll say I don't care for some of them, but she always says, if it's business, who's fussy? Like to have your food out in the bar? That's popular by day.'

'Thanks, yes. It'll be fine out there.'

I went back but as I entered the bar I saw one of the fishermen was standing by our table, talking to Helen Jane as if he knew her well. It looked a serious discussion. I took my time reaching the table so as not to interrupt.

He looked up, saw me, nodded and then shrugged his shoulders slightly as he turned away from her. He went back to the bar.

'That was a friend who has obliged me from time to time,' she said. 'He just told me he fished up a shot conger this morning. Very curious. Shot in two places by two bullets from an automatic rifle.'

'A big conger,' I said drily. 'But how does he know so much about rifles?'

'He was in the Marines. I think he's on Reserve. He knows shots all right. He wouldn't be mistaken.'

'Where did he catch it?'

'Off the Wiseman Creek,' she said. 'Someone must have been testing his firearm last night.'

'He knows it was last night?'

'He was born a fisherman.'

'Why did he tell you?'

'He said he had heard a rumour about a gun-running ship going through yesterday. Hove-to twelve miles out with a sick man aboard. A helicopter went and took him off. He says the Irish are waiting to make an arrest because they've had wind of the guns aboard.'

'Do you think they're aboard?' I said very quietly.

'I really don't know. But the Irish will find out very soon.'

'And he told you because he's also had wind your brother might have something to do with it,' I said.

'I think he just mentioned the shot

conger as an interest item,' she said calmly. 'It went on from there.'

'Did you know your cook was an agent for Mail Order houses?'

'Not shot congers by post, surely?' She smiled.

'The man in the corner of the bar is watching us in that wall mirror,' I said. 'Do you know him?'

There was a pause until she had a chance to take a long look.

'Louis Fertiller,' she said. 'On the Council. Supposed to watch the foreshore and cliffs for any dangers along this stretch of coast. Believed by local people to be a Customs nark.'

'The vultures are gathering,' I said, looking out of the window.

'Is that really what you feel?' she said.

'Yes. I see trouble in every approaching cloud. Better enjoy your food when it comes. Disaster ruins the palate.'

'While I'm down here, there is something I might as well do. She won't be ready yet.'

'About half an hour, she said.'

She nodded and went out on to the

hard. I saw her walk quickly away to the left towards the half moon of cottages and three small shops.

I felt sure it was not some small item of shopping she had remembered, but a need to go out after hearing the story of the shot conger.

It was still squirming in my head that she was queen of the gun runners and that the ex-marine, at least, knew it.

George came over and briefly laid a table. He looked pale and uneasy.

'I must have eaten something,' he confided. 'Had a bad night. Wife got fed up and parked herself in the sitting room. I could only sleep a few minutes at a time. Can't think what it was.'

'There's a lot of it about,' I said, unsympathetically.

'Unless somebody spiked me drink,' he said, very confidentially. He stared at me with such intensity that his eyes bulged like bloodshot boiled eggs.

'But then you'd have slept,' I said.

'Ah-h-h!' he said as if considering a great discovery. 'Yes, I suppose I would of.'

He went away. I sat and waited, looking through a diary to pretend to be occupied. H.J.'s going made me uneasy, but I hadn't realised it immediately. The unease increased as the minutes passed.

Julie came in and looked towards me. She cocked her head in question when she saw I was alone.

'She won't be long,' I said. 'I'll wait.'

'Okay,' she said.

The minutes passed. I looked at my watch. She had been gone almost half an hour. I went through to the kitchen.

'I think she's got lost,' I said. 'I'll go and look.'

'She wouldn't get lost in a maze,' Julie said, staring at me. 'You want me to keep this in the slow oven? Don't leave it too long.'

'I'll be as quick as I can. She may be talking to somebody.'

'Never been known,' she said, drily.

'What do you mean by that?'

'She wouldn't talk to anybody down here. The high and mighty Wisemans never did, never will. She must have had a bloody good reason to come in here, and

I'd like to know what it is.'

'Well, I don't know. I'm just carrying out a business assignment. She is a stranger to me. Just hold it, will you?'

She looked quizzical but said nothing.

The only men who watched while I crossed the bar to go out was the man by the mirror and George. George watched morosely, as if he wished it was he going out.

The air was quite fresh. Outside the harbour the sea was grey-green, heavily streaked with white horses. Two or three people were walking on the hard. Half a dozen cars were parked, but the whole place looked as if it had retired into its shell till next Spring, when the holiday season would start again.

I walked along looking up the narrow alleys I passed, but saw nothing of her. I went into all three shops and bought some small thing that came to mind as an excuse for calling.

The feeling came upon me first, that she had done a bunk. That is inelegantly put, but I thought that it had been inelegantly done.

As I came to the end of the village and turned back, the arresting thought came that she had gone out on her own account and had walked into a trap.

I did not know exactly why anyone in the village should want to grab her, but by then I had enough suspicions that might justify the move.

At that time I was undecided, frankly because I did not want to believe that she had been kidnapped.

I walked all over that tiny village and saw nothing of her. More important, I saw no sign of anybody watching me, which I would expect in the circumstances.

She might have gone back to the inn by the back way, I thought, quickening my pace. I could have been getting too fearful.

But when I got back into the bar, she was not there.

Nor was the customs nark.

And the men who had not bothered to watch me go, were obviously curious when I came back.

9

The disappearance of Helen Jane Wiseman at that time and in that place started my mind tracking away from the course it had been trying to hold until then.

She had gone deliberately, I felt. The coincidence of the customs nark leaving soon after seemed to add to the importance of her going.

I went through the bar into the passage again and so to the kitchen.

'I'm sorry. I can't find her,' I said.

'Okay. I'll do something with it,' Julie said, 'don't worry. I know her by reputation.'

George shouted something from the bar. She understood it, apparently, though I didn't. She shouted back.

'Bit difficult, I suppose, just the two of you managing the pub and the cooking and the rooms.' I made it sound sympathetic.

'Well, it's only three weeks in the year,'

she said. 'It's not that bad.'

I thought it probably wasn't that bad with George helping himself from morning till night from the bar stock.

'We do all right from it,' she said, with a wink. 'Perks here and there on the food ordering and that.'

Like her sister, the Cook I thought. Perhaps food fiddling on a small scale was a family racket the sisters shared in.

'She may have gone back to the house,' I said, looking at my watch. 'I suppose I'd better go up there. She's a difficult woman to do business with.'

'So they say,' she said drily.

'Have you seen Mr McGuffy? I gave him a lift. It was a lonely place. I wondered if he got back.'

'Oh yes, he was in,' she said.

'Oh good,' I said through a partially locked throat. 'When?'

'Oh, about an hour back. Had a Guinness and went. Funny chap. Always dreaming about something, I reckon.'

'Right. Sorry, again. I'll be back later,' I said, and almost added, 'I hope.'

I went past the counter to my table and

finished my drink. The ex-Marine was standing quite close, throwing darts at a board on the wall.

'Difficult woman, that,' he said quietly.

I looked at the dartboard.

'Purposeful,' I said.

'You're a stranger hereabout,' he said. 'Take some advice. Don't turn your back.'

He went to get the darts out of the board. I finished my drink and left.

McGuffy is back, I thought as I unlocked the car. If he was, why show himself at the pub? Just to show he was back, as if somebody might doubt he was alive if he didn't show.

I drove off up the hill to the road which ran along the side of the Ravenleigh estate and on to the cross-roads, where I turned down to the boathouse.

The attitude of the man I had seen on the workshop floor down there had been of a dead man. The posture was unmistakable.

As I drove I recounted my actions in the seconds after McGuffy had charged the door in. There could have been time for him to fall with the door and jump up again, supposing he had seen someone standing out on the gallery above the shop.

Supposing further he had chucked that person over the rails and then hidden himself?

It was possible. I had been wary and therefore slow in passing through the office and going out to the gallery.

He could have done those things, but it was odd that the man down on the floor should have looked exactly the same as he did.

When I switched off the engine by the side of the boathouse, there seemed to be a few seconds of silence before I again heard the hushing of the water amongst the piles of the landing stage in front of the building.

There was no surprise in finding nothing had been moved since I'd gone. The office was in the same dreary mess. I walked over the fallen door and went on to the gallery.

I'm not sure exactly, but I think it was then that I had the feeling that someone was watching me. I looked behind me, through the office and across the boarded landing stage to the bushes and trees beyond it. I know it was when I got on the gallery that I actually looked back, but I may have had the feeling of being watched when I arrived there.

There was nothing to be seen of anyone. I turned and looked down to the shop floor. The man was still there.

Once more I looked behind me, then carefully around the roof trusses and the inside of the wooden building, but saw no one.

The fact was I had seen no one the first time, but it seemed to me that someone must have been there then, presumably McGuffy.

I went down the wooden steps. The man was lying on the floor beside one of the stocked boats. The old denim jacket and jeans were the same washed out blue, shabby rough edged as McGuffy's. The hair was fair but it appeared the man had rolled over in the dust and yellow shavings, which clung to his head.

I bent down by him, took a handful of hair and lifted his head so I could see his face. His face was a mess of blood as if he had smashed his nose in.

Possibly he had been standing directly behind the door when McGuffy had smashed it in. In which case, the door must have turned round as it crashed between the two of them.

There was no point in guessing just what had happened in the seconds after that collision. Perhaps he had run, blinded by his hurt and had just gone head-long over the gallery rails.

In the back of the tight jeans was a wallet just showing in the pocket top. I used a handkerchief to ease it out, and looked inside.

There was a motor insurance certificate in the name of Helen Jane Wiseman; a driver's licence in the name of James Ralph Mercer and some money.

I put the wallet back where it had been and stood up.

There was no doubt in my mind the dead man had been the chauffeur-handyman at Ravenleigh.

Things were beginning to form a pattern at last. The factotum and Cook were dead. The brother was dead. The whole murder scene was a house affair.

But murder?

What reason I had to assume it was murder I don't know, but it made me bend down again, and this time I very carefully pulled up one shoulder so I could see the man's chest.

He had been shot. I let the body down again.

Either McGuffy had had a gun or there had been a third man in the boatshed then.

The only sounds in that place as I stood by the body were the sucking and gurgle of water under parts of the floor. The boat in the dock moved restlessly as I watched, but its ties made no creaking.

I went round the place. It was an untidy workshop, tools left around, planks, beams stacked haphazardly against the walls, ply sheets leaning against walls so they sagged from their own weight. Wood and plastic offcuts were lying around everywhere.

It was clearly a workshop for slap-up running repairs; plug the hole, patch it and send it to sea again till something better could be done — but not in this place.

I went to the speed boat in the dock, reached over and folded back part of the canvas cover to the driver's seat. Lying along the seat beside the wheel was an automatic rifle.

There was no point in hanging about. I went back to my car.

Cook was dead — although I realised then that I did not know for sure — and Jim had been dead since ten a.m. He had not gone to the wedding; that was certain, and Cook had not gone, either.

In that case, had any of them gone? A cook's maid had to be married and Helen's maid had been to go with her, both driven by Jim, who hadn't gone.

Where were the maids?

Depression grew thicker over my head as I drove up the hill. I went in at the gates and drove round the house to the back. I got some tools from my car and got into the rear of Cook's. With some difficulty I got the back of the rear seat half away from the boot.

As I did that I heard a terrified breath, and then a whimpering, a desperate gasp for breath and then a shout of 'Help!'

As the seat folded down I looked in. A distant face looked at me and started to scream.

'It's all right,' I said. 'Stop that! Stop it! You're all right!'

It was not a fat woman. It was a girl.

★ ★ ★

Getting her out was very difficult. For a while she struggled against me and then fought to get out on her own and made a mess of both until she ran out of breath and rested.

'I — can't! I'm all — bent up — ' she gasped.

'Rest a minute, then I'll give you a hand.'

'It's panic,' she said. 'I'm claustrophobic. Frightened, I can't get out!'

'The way you're doubled in there, I think it's best to let me have your legs and I'll hold so you can push against the back of the boot lid. I can't pull much.

179

There isn't room.'

'Boot lid? Am I in a boot?' She swore very strongly. 'Right. I feel calmer now I know where I am. I thought I was down a drain smelling of petrol. Grab my ankles.'

The girl did not sound like a maid, but I left the difficulty of identification until I had got her out. Once I got her legs free and pulled she began to come out like a backward beetle. I got out of the door while she completed the scramble.

I helped her out to the ground. She stood there straight and tall and flushed — too flushed, because she burst into tears and grabbed me for a shoulder.

She went on crying as if getting rid of a week's nightmares in one great gale. I held her, of course, and patted and soothed, not without pleasure, until the storm subsided.

'Thank you,' she said and sniffed. 'I feel so awful. I think I've been doped.'

'Let me see your arms.'

She showed me.

'You've had two jabs. Remember anything?'

'Remember anything — ?' She shook

her head, frowning as if about to cry again. 'I don't even know where I am!'

She looked round, then over the car to the house.

'Oh lord, I'm home!' She leaned against the roof and just shook her head again. 'I can't think. I just want to die or something. I feel awful.'

'Come and sit in my car for a minute or two. It's shock and I think I woke you before the dope gave out.'

I led her to my car and she sat in it, still slightly shaking her head every now and then and closing her eyes tightly. She was very young.

Quite suddenly I thought: this must be Helen Jane's daughter.

'I'm a friend of your mother,' I said. 'I came to help her in a private matter. She has gone out for a while.'

She did not listen but began to cry again.

'I feel terrible! I wish I was dead — '

'Your mother,' I said, trying to get in through the black fog of the departing drug. 'I was telling you — '

'Oh, mother, mother!' she said, pitifully

but pointlessly. She scrummaged in the pocket of her raincoat and brought out a ball of paper which she shoved into my hand, then fell along the seat and really let go at crying.

I undid the paper ball. It was a letter from Helen Jane dated two days before.

'Darling,
    Don't come home just now, and please don't telephone. I'm perfectly all right but having trouble with the staff and everything is in a mess. I will come up to you next week,
                              Love,
                                Mother.'

This was a different sort of Helen from the one I had found so far. It was a different story from the one she had given me to swallow.

She had never seemed the one to 'have trouble with the staff'. I should have thought the staff wouldn't have lasted through five minutes of any trouble with her.

But what made it quite clear that such

trouble did exist was that sentence which ended, 'and please don't telephone'. That made it sound as if her calls were being intercepted by the staff.

It sounded, in fact, as if the staff were in command at the house.

She had given them time to go to a wedding, she said. Had she? Clearly they hadn't gone because the driver who was to have taken them had never gone and the second car was standing by me at that moment.

So what was the purpose of that yarn? The idea that she had feared the staff knew of the brother's murder did not work, because the letter had been written on the day he died, and as I had already noted locally, the last post went from the village at 4.35 pm.

She couldn't have kept the room shut off for longer than she had without rousing the staff's suspicion to full strength.

I looked at the girl. She had stopped crying and seemed to have fallen asleep on the seat. I thought it best to let her rest until her head cleared.

But the urgency of the position she had brought with her was pressing. She had been doped and locked in the boot of Cook's car. There must have been an intention to dispose of her in some way when the attackers came back to Cook's car.

And when they came back they wouldn't find it where it had been left. Then if they looked round the back of the house they would find the car, myself and the girl.

It was a nasty position and it again raised the question of what had happened to Helen Jane.

I crossed to Cook's car, pushed the rear seat back to where it should have been, and shut the doors. I came back to my car and drove away with the girl asleep on the back seat. It seemed essential to get away from the house until the girl was awake and fit to tell how she got shoved into that car boot.

I knew what I was asking for when I drove out of the gates. The people against us were those interested in guns by the dozen and large quantities of drugs. If I had suspected even a tenth of such opposition, I would never have come within two hundred miles of this wretched place.

As it was I should be lucky ever to see any place two hundred miles from here again. It made me very sad, restless and very angry.

Very suddenly she said, 'Where are we going? I want to go home!'

I pulled into a layby by some trees. It was about five miles from Ravenleigh.

'Just riding around till you came to,' I said, turning my head. 'Do you feel better yet?'

'I feel awful, but I don't want to die any more. Where are we? What are you doing?'

'Let me ask you,' I said. 'How did you get in that car boot?'

'I don't know,' she said and frowned, then shook her head.

'You couldn't have been picked up by accident,' I said. 'Did you get home?'

'No. No, I didn't. I hitched down from school, you see — ' She looked at me suddenly. 'Are you a friend of Mother's?'

'I told you. I'm her professional adviser. It's a legal matter.'

'Oh, I see.'

'Well, you didn't get home. So you hitched somewhere, and then rang up home?'

'Yes, that's right. I got to Mark's Cross — that's about twenty miles. I was dead beat, really. And I was so near I thought if I rang she had to come, no matter what she said to me afterwards.'

'Did she come?' I said, surprised.

'No, Cook took the call. She said, Oh poor lamb, you must be frozen, or something like that, and said Mother was still asleep so she'd come and bring hot coffee — '

She stopped and shrugged.

'So she came, you drank the coffee from her flask and went to sleep,' I said. 'Why did the letter worry you so much that you went against your mother's advice?'

'I had a feeling — ' She shrugged again as if unable to explain further.

'But the letter hardly says anything,' I said. 'In fact, the only thing it says is about trouble with the staff. Is that what worried you?'

She looked frightened. It came over her quickly, as if she had suddenly remembered something terrifying.

'Yes,' she said very quietly.

'Why? What had ever happened to make you nervous of them?'

She shook her head but said nothing.

'It would be best if you went back to school,' I said. 'You know that? I am at Ravenleigh on your mother's behalf, and I will stay until she is free of anything that worries her. That's what I'm here for. If she finds out you came and what happened, she will be so worried she might do something she will regret later. Can you understand that?'

She nodded.

'I'm sorry I came,' she said in a whisper.

'You ought to be grateful nothing else happened to you,' I said. 'I'll take you to the train. There's a direct line up from here.'

'Yes. I usually — But I haven't any money. Not enough.'

'I have. Don't worry about that.'

I waited with her at the station until the train came in and put her aboard with enough money for food and a car the other end. She was very grateful, but had started to be frightened of what had happened to her in the last few hours and just wanted to be away and back at school and friends and safety.

I watched the train go right out. A few people had got on or off, but I really did not expect any interference with the girl once the train had left.

When I went back into the station yard, other cars, which had come to meet the train had gone, and mine was alone out there.

It seemed symbolic, to my melo-dramatic mind, of the fight of one man against a surrounding wall of unseen enemies. I felt almost elated by the nobility of my position until I got into the car and went to switch on.

By accident or lucky interference, I had cut across the path of the villains. They would now be looking for me. It would be crazy to go back there. After all, the safety of mankind did not depend on my help. I had a good life which went wrong on occasion, but in the main suited me. Why, for Heaven's sake, walk back to Ravenleigh into the possibility of my pleasurable life being curtailed?

But Helen Jane was, when I came to think, not easily discarded. In fact, I did not think I wanted to discard her until I had forced her to be eternally grateful to me.

Further, I had not been paid.

I began to drive away, very slowly.

10

As I came near the grounds of Ravenleigh it was grey afternoon. The wind was beginning to move up in the higher trees and dead leaves were falling with a little skeleton rattle as they dropped through their fellows still hanging on.

I heard these things clearly for I had pulled into the wood and switched off to sort out my immediate future.

The return to the house was likely to be fraught with interest, for I was sure the staff would be back and by that time they would have found the girl gone from the car boot, so they would know that something had gone wrong for them.

Though there was no reason why they should suspect me if I arrived — they had never seen me, as far as I could tell — they might be so put out as to suspect anybody.

At that time, determined, against my will, to get back into the house and to

Helen Jane, I fully believed that turning up as the innocent legal adviser would turn suspicion away from me.

There was a possibility that, on my first visit to the house, one of the staff had seen me without my seeing them, but I had left the house quite shortly after, which should have made everything seem above board.

The real danger was that I might have been seen being shown into the murder room, but I was quite sure that Helen Jane had cleared anyone out of the vicinity by one order or another which would have taken each one of them right away.

No, as I looked at the prospect in the quiet of the wood I saw no reason for being suspected on my return except for the raw state of my own nerves.

In any case, after all the arguing with myself, I really wanted to find out what had happened to Helen Jane, and if she had fallen into deep trouble, and then to find a way to get her out before she was cancelled out.

Possibly, what made me persuade

myself so easily was that I knew Jim, the chauffeur handyman, was dead, and the rest of the staff comprised three women. The gardener, as I had understood, was a part time fellow who came in from somewhere else. I was sure Helen Jane would not have engaged him to come in while such dangerous things were happening in and around the house.

So I reckoned on three women. Dangerous women, almost certainly, because a lot of money was behind all this, but women.

I cannot think now why I felt some relief in that, because most of my past difficulties have been caused by the demands of women. However, in some cases decision is subservient to optimism, specially when the optimism is based purely on something one wants.

I started up. Three women! Heavens above, a day ago I was scared of a sable coat and had conquered the fear.

. I drove in through the gates and pulled up by the terrace. In the car locker I keep a small, expensive briefcase which adds to the fraudulence of my presentation.

It contains a small twenty-two calibre pistol which is not in the least pretentious.

With the briefcase in hand I approached the front door. There was no sign of life about, nor any movement of someone peering from a window.

I came to the door and put out my hand to the bellpush, then noticed that the door was not shut. It was open an inch or more. I pushed and it opened easily.

The hall was empty. I went in, then remembering my innocence, turned back and rang the bell. I heard it down the long passage as I stood in the hall, holding my case in both hands, apparently waiting with professional patience.

What looked like Julie came out through the passage door. As she came closer I saw it was not, but it was very like her.

'Miss Wiseman is away,' she said, firmly. 'I'm sorry.' I looked surprised.

'Away? But I was with her not two hours ago. She asked me to come again this afternoon! You'll forgive me, but I'm rather bewildered.'

She looked very curiously at me.

'What is your business?' she said.

'It's a legal matter,' I said. 'I understood she would complete it this afternoon. Why on earth did she suddenly go like that?'

I could see a small sign that Cook was taken aback by what I had said, but more by the 'legal matter' than by the rest of it.

'Well, that's what she said,' Cook explained, and looked behind her. 'I could see if she's gone yet.'

'If you would. It would be a complete waste of my journey if she has gone. I came a long way.'

I had the feeling she knew that. Probably Julie had told her I was staying at the pub. She and Julie were in business together on side affairs, I remembered; the matter of working fiddles on food, and probably other swindles as well.

She turned and went up the main staircase to the top, then went out of sight.

Food, heroin, guns; the fishing village; the boathouse; it was suddenly quite clear what connected the lot.

There were no dealers in drugs or guns here. They were all local people. That was why the village had watched me, been interested in me and what I had to do with the Big House.

They were smugglers. That was it. They were not dealers in anything. They brought stuff in, no matter what it was, and were paid for doing that and for nothing else.

There were no armed gangs; the ambush had been to get the evidence of smuggling away from me and the evidence of murder right away from the village.

That angle of it was not so different from the one I had seen at first, except in one very serious respect.

Dealers in drugs or guns would be dangerous but numerically small. With smuggling, the whole village could be interested in seeing I didn't blow the industry.

Smuggling was one of the original cottage industries; it had made villages prosperous, kept families together. It was an industry which kept pace with the age. Tea, tobacco, spirits, had all had their times when most in demand and now drugs and guns and other illegal essentials had taken the place of the tea chest and the keg of brandy.

Smuggling brought things for which people would pay, but it also brought violence, murder and sudden death.

I realised then that I had been very foolish to come back. The sensible thing to do was turn and go right away, but the village could be alerted before I could get away from the vicinity of the house. The villagers could block many roads.

Having come so far in it might be sensible to join them, but I felt they wouldn't take alien recruits.

With no one in sight and in the quiet peace of that house I had the feeling I was trapped all round, and no matter which way I tried to go, someone would be there barring my way.

Cook appeared at the top of the stairs.

'Would you like to come up?' she said, and smiled.

I think that because she smiled I knew

that something was wrong, but if I didn't stick to my role of innocence I wouldn't get out of the place as soon as I had hoped.

I smiled back and went upstairs, the briefcase under my left arm, in which place it serves much the same convenience as a shoulder holster.

Cook waited for me at the top, but her smile had gone. She even looked a little worried, and if she were half as worried as I was then, I could have felt some sympathy.

★　★　★

She turned when I got to her and the way she turned was towards the brother's bedroom. My inner tension increased as we walked over the deep carpet to the door.

She turned to it, turned the handle and pushed the door slightly in. I felt I had to keep out of that room, though I did not know why.

'This surely is a bedroom?' I said.

'It is.' She looked impatient. 'You

wanted to see Miss Wiseman?'

'Yes. But I am sorry. In my profession one must be circumspect.'

She stood quite still by the partly open door. My objection had taken her aback. She had not thought of such a protest; but then I had only that moment chosen it out of desperation.

'Unless you accompany me?' I said.

She stood there solid, suspicious.

'She would not have that for confidential business. She is not in the bed.'

'Then why does she not come to the door?' I said, trying to keep a sober, stupid line.

'Do you want to see her, or don't you?'

I took the initiative then and called out loudly and very clearly.

'Miss Wiseman! May I speak with you?'

Cook slammed the door. I recognised that the bang signalled the end of the game on both sides. She came towards me, then stopped as I put a hand towards her.

'What have you done to Miss Wiseman?' I said, then put my hand back on top of the briefcase.

Her alarm was obvious, but for an instant she looked past me and showed brief relief at what she saw. Cook was not an actress.

I stepped aside until my back was to the wall with Cook on my left and the stairs on my right.

There was a woman standing at the top of the stairs, pointing a rifle at me. From the way she altered aim to follow my quick dodge, I gathered she had been about to shoot me in the back.

I pulled out my little pistol and fired it towards her, hitting the ceiling. She was so surprised she all but dropped the rifle.

'Put it on the floor and come out where I can see all of you,' I said.

She obeyed in such a way that I realised she was inexperienced with the handling of guns, but it was still lucky for me she hadn't noticed how rusty my shooting was. That the shot had hit the ceiling was what I had intended but I was so out of practice I wasn't too sure where on the ceiling it would go.

Cook stood quite still but her eyes flicked from my gun to my face very anxiously indeed. The other woman came slowly, wary I would fire again. She was a scraggy looking creature but very, very angry.

'Sit on those chairs against the wall. Both of you.'

They did that, one each side of the table which had held the plain wooden coffin of the murdered man.

'Where is Miss Wiseman?' I said.

'She is at school,' Cook said sharply.

'The younger Miss Wiseman is on her way back,' I said. 'I put her on the train.'

They were surprised and angrier still.

'Is there anything else you should know?' I said. 'Oh yes! Your chauffeur Jim.'

'Where is he?' Cook said, increasingly alarmed.

'Dead,' I said. 'I found his body in the Wiseman boathouse. He had been murdered.'

There was a stunned silence. I could see shock in their faces, then fear, but no sort of sentimental concern.

'Who else is in the house?' I said.

'Hurry up answering. I don't intend to waste time.'

Cook looked coolly at me and almost smiled.

'Five,' she said. 'And there's certain to be more when they know you're here.'

'Oh, don't worry about me,' I said, trying to sound casual. 'I'm not interested in smuggling.'

Cook drew in a sharp breath, making a hiss. The other woman muttered something.

'I'm in favour of private industry,' I said. 'All I want is Miss Wiseman, and I might as well tell you why. I want my pay. Now do you understand?'

When I said it like that and as I had a gun, I was sure they accepted the idea that I was not some kind of law man, but some kind of crook, like themselves but in a different branch.

'Money,' said the thin woman, curiously. 'Oh, it's like that, is it? We were all beginning to wonder, just about little things — '

'Oh, shut up. You wonder about anybody,' Cook said.

I was pleased with the reaction to my explanation, but an idea crept into my mind that they were seeming to agree in order to waste time.

Then I thought that Cook had meant me to go in that bedroom, and it became my turn to wonder if someone was waiting for me in there.

It may have been telepathy, because about a half minute later I saw the door move very slightly. I raised the gun, pointing it at the door.

'Tell me what makes you wonder about Miss Wiseman,' I said. 'Do you wonder if she is broke?'

The door opened a little more. I guessed that if somebody did come out it would be with a gun pointed at me. There were a lot of guns somewhere sprinkled around the area, and no licences were needed.

Whoever was behind the door was someone appointed to duff me up, or perhaps do me altogether. As far as murder went, that room was lucky for murderers.

No one came out. The door must have

opened just enough for anyone inside to see out, then very slowly and silently, it began to close again.

The watcher had seen me with the gun in my hand and had been dissuaded from coming out to challenge.

Or perhaps gone back to get reinforcements.

'Right,' I told the women. 'Tell me where she is.'

'I didn't see her. My sister said she was down there with you. At the pub. She must have gone off.'

'Let's go and look in her bedroom,' I said.

'You said you wouldn't go in there,' Cook said, with a small grim smile.

'I said her room this time,' I explained. 'The one you took me to is her brother's. Don't try and hedge on me. I know enough to fix the pair of you and all your friends for ten years of the best, and that's with remission.

'And further,' I said, in a flash of inspiration, 'to try and keep me quiet is a waste of time. When I put the daughter on the train I rang my office in London and recorded everything on my computer tape. If I don't turn up to stop it within twenty-four hours, it automatically sends out the whole recording to all enquiry agents and police headquarters.'

I felt such a lift at my genius that I almost added, 'And that should make you understand I am not a small man.'

The women got up and turned down the corridor past the stairs. They began to go towards Helen Jane's room. I followed, but on the way looked back to the brother's door and down the stairs as they came into view.

No one showed either way. I picked up the rifle.

They stopped at the door.

'She isn't here,' Cook said.

'Just let's look, in case she came back and you didn't see her.'

'You say Jim's murdered,' the scraggy woman said. 'Who done that?'

'Man called McGuffy,' I said. 'Didn't Julie tell you about him?'

'That's another — that's two of 'em around,' the thin woman said in some agitation. 'It's her! She's brought them in.

I told you, Em, I told you! You said we could take over when he got done, but it don't look too much like that now!'

'There's nothing worse than trying to cook for bloody lunatics,' Cook said, looking at me as if for agreement. 'One stolen pig and you'd think the Mafia had moved in. Well, look here,' she snapped. turning to the other woman, 'Jim may have stolen the pig and he may not, but what's it now? We'm eaten him so it's too late to cry now!'

'Open that door,' I said. 'And don't waste any more time talking rubbish.'

I could not have opened it myself, even if they weren't very close because I had the pistol in one hand and the rifle and briefcase handle in the other. To ease the burden I let the case drop. Open at the top it hit the floor with a hearty slap. The thin woman jumped and almost screamed with fright, then pushed Cook aside and tried to open the door.

'Oh — ! It's locked, it's locked!' she shouted, in such a frenzy she must have thought I would shoot her if she didn't open it. 'She's locked it!'

Cook, still firmly calm, shoved the thin one aside and tried the door for herself.

'It is locked,' she said, and was so surprised she took no further notice of the gun at her back and knocked on the panels with her fist. 'Open up! You can't get out of there!'

'Miss Wiseman!' I called out for the second time. 'Can you hear me?'

There was silence. Even the two women were holding their breaths, as if they feared there might be an answer.

As we waited I wondered why 'she' could not get out of the room. If she could not get out any other way, why lock herself in thereby making her own prison?

'She's not in there,' I said. 'Unless you've killed her, too.'

Cook turned slowly and stared at me. She seemed to stare for a long time without moving, while the thin woman stared at her.

'You know a lot,' Cook said. 'But some of it's wrong. I didn't kill Wiseman. I had no cause. Jim did. He had a cause. He did all the work, ran the boats, repairs, brought the stuff in, and all he got was his pay.'

'If he had a grouse it wasn't worth murder,' I said.

'It wasn't like that. It was a row. A big row. There was thousands coming in down there in the river. Thousands. But Wiseman checked everything so Jim couldn't rake off for himself. That was the start of it.

'Then he got a contact that wanted guns. Jim got 'em in. That night Wiseman found out and that was what the row was about. Wiseman didn't want guns. They brought trouble. Anyhow — they argued, and that was it.'

She shrugged.

Then McGuffy killed Jim, I thought. So what was McGuffy? A self appointed policeman, judge, hangman? He must have known about that murder when he arrived, and the ringing of that damned bell a ploy to disturb us. In the end he must have seen us through the fanlight over the door, handling the arms box, then got into the room by the balcony.

Once he'd seen the room cleaned up,

he must have known what the game was on our part.

'Where did Jim hide the guns?' I said.

'They were in the tomb. They had to be shifted — because of what you were doing — '

'You attacked when we were moving the box?'

She shrugged again.

'Men from the village,' she said. 'Never leave any mess lying round. My fishermen don't leave their guts on the beach.'

'What did you get involved for?' the thin woman said, sharply.

'Money,' I said, with warm honesty.

I heard voices in the hall below.

'Who's that?' I whispered.

'The men,' Cook said. 'There's five. I told you.'

I remembered there should have been another woman.

'Was there a wedding?' I said.

'Oh yes,' Cook said. 'Just happened the place had the same name as another one up in Gloucester. Miss took the wrong one.'

'With your help.' I listened. The voices

seemed to be drawing away somewhere. 'Where is Miss Helen?'

'She's supposed to be in here,' Cook said. 'Perhaps there's a way out.'

I knew that if one fired at a lock it opened, but that was on the films. I did not know what part of the lock to hit, or what was supposed to happen when it was hit.

To call out again would be to call up the defenders from below. I did not want to see them. As an agency man I have been an investigator, not a thick ear specialist. Situations like this were not for me. All I was able to concentrate on was how to get out safely.

But I couldn't get out with the men downstairs.

'You thought the door would be unlocked, so she was tied up or knocked out when you put her in?' I said.

'Trussed,' said Cook.

'You captured her and knocked out the girl — what's going to happen that these two had to be out of the way?'

'There was a business deal — '

She stopped and looked up. So did I.

So did the thin woman.

From outside there came the screech and scream of several cars pulling in. It sounded like six or seven. There were shouts of alarm from the men downstairs.

I pushed the women away from the door and fired a shot into the lock just as a burst of firing came from outside. The door opened. I ran into the room. All the curtains were drawn back. Helen Jane was sitting up on the bed.

I delayed her rescue for several seconds while I went to one window and looked down. Behind me the women were calling to the men below and as I glanced back I saw them running for the stairs.

It was like a scene from a film down by the terrace. Four cars were pulled up at all angles on the grass and men were running from them across the terrace; men with machine rifles and woolly hats pulled down over their faces.

My knees felt weak and I turned away to untie Helen Jane, who looked very uncomfortable. As I sawed the cords with my penknife, I heard the row downstairs.

It sounded like fighting. There was

thudding, shouting, grunting and crash-ing of furniture. It brought sweat to my brow.

I got her free. She just sat on the bed rubbing her ankles and looking at me curiously. I looked at the door anxiously.

The sounds of fighting stopped as if one side had won. We heard brief orders being shouted and other sounds of orderly action.

Then, 'Okay! Out!'

I went back to the window. The attackers were going out again, carrying boxes of the sort we had cased Wiseman into. It was all highly organised, I could see, and the man who seemed to be organising with nods of his shock head wore jeans and appeared as interested in rolling a cigarette as in watching his troops carry out the arms.

He raised a hand. A man near the door below nodded and shouted one word. Men jerked into fast action. The boxes were loaded in the cars, the door the men disappeared inside, doors slammed, the cars slewed away across the grass and raced for the gate.

Three more cars sped round from the back of the house and followed on to the procession.

The cars pulled out and away. McGuffy took a last look up at the house and then walked up the drive to the gates, still rolling his cigarette.

I was so glad I hadn't been downstairs when the attack was on.

She stood up.

'It was very painful,' she said.

'You shouldn't have walked out on me.'

'My dear sleuth, when the man said two bullets in a conger it was actually meaning in me, so I went in the hope of being spared if I did what I was told. I was tumbled into a car, brought back here and left in here. That lock shuts by itself.

'Do you know, you were right, when you said that guns could bring unpleasant people.'

'Well, I'm quite sure that the lot who just took them, didn't pay for them. Do you think your staff and their friends are all dead?' I spoke diffidently because I didn't want to go downstairs and find out.

'I only heard firing at the start. After that it seemed like close encounter work, as they call it — '

She broke off. We heard voices below. They were more like mumbles followed by confused sounds of movement, then silence.

When we did go down, after a while, the house was deserted by staff. We were alone, just the two of us.

'I'm going to bed,' she said. 'Come along.'

As we turned we saw a car coming up the drive quite clearly because the fracas had left the front door wide open.

'Who the hell's this?' said Helen Jane.

The car stopped. The door opened. A sable coat got out very gracefully, but determinedly.

I stood and considered the pros and cons of my position. The smugglers had lost their guns, and perhaps some other merchandise intended for private sale, but they might easily suspect that I, the stranger, might have been the lookout for the commandos. It did not seem circumspect to stay and find out. Though I felt I would miss Helen Jane, I could always send her the bill 'For Cleaning Services' later. Meanwhile the better place for me was away from Ravenleigh and the village, even costing my small amount of luggage left at the inn.

'I said, who the hell is it?' Helen Jane said angrily.

'It's the Cavalry,' I said, and went to the door to meet the sable coat.

THE END

We do hope that you have enjoyed reading this large print book.

Did you know that all of our titles are available for purchase?

We publish a wide range of high quality large print books including:
**Romances, Mysteries, Classics
General Fiction
Non Fiction and Westerns**

Special interest titles available in large print are:
**The Little Oxford Dictionary
Music Book, Song Book
Hymn Book, Service Book**

Also available from us courtesy of Oxford University Press:
**Young Readers' Dictionary
(large print edition)
Young Readers' Thesaurus
(large print edition)**

For further information or a free brochure, please contact us at:
**Ulverscroft Large Print Books Ltd.,
The Green, Bradgate Road, Anstey,
Leicester, LE7 7FU, England.
Tel:** (00 44) **0116 236 4325**
Fax: (00 44) **0116 234 0205**

Other titles in the
Linford Mystery Library:

DEATH SQUAD

Basil Copper

Lost in a fog on National Forest terrain, Mike Faraday, the laconic L.A. private investigator, hears shots. A dying man staggers out of the bushes. Paul Dorn, a brilliant criminal lawyer, is quite dead when Mike gets to him. So how could he be killed again in a police shoot-out in L.A. the same night? The terrifying mystery into which Faraday is plunged convinces him that a police death squad is involved. The problem is solved only in the final, lethal shoot-out.

DEAD RECKONING

George Douglas

After a large-scale post office robbery, expert peterman Edgar Mulley's fingerprints are found on a safe and he lands in jail. The money has never been recovered, and three years later Mulley makes a successful break for freedom. The North Central Regional Crime Squad lands the case when a 'grasser' gets information to them. But before Chief Superintendent Hallam and Inspector 'Jack' Spratt can interrogate the informer, he is found dead. Then, a second mysterious death occurs . . .

THE SILENT INFORMER

P. A. Foxall

A man found murdered in a quiet street brings the police a crop of unpleasant problems. But when the victim is found to have a criminal record, an affluent lifestyle, and no visible honest means of support, the problems proliferate. It seems there could be a lot of villains who wanted him dead. The Catford detectives suddenly find themselves immersed in new enquiries into apparently unrelated crimes of two years ago, which can now be seen to add up to a murderous conspiracy.